FULL DISCLOSURE

VEILED INTENTIONS
BOOK 4

ELLE KEATON

NIALL

The ring of Niall's cell phone was jarring and interrupted the blissful peace and priceless quiet he'd finally achieved. The morning had been set aside to review the details of an unsolved J. Doe case the West Coast Forensics team was working on. While he liked his husband's niece, Riley, and his mother-in-law, Alyson, they were talkers, and they'd only left a few minutes ago after unexpectedly stopping by to drop off home-made treats for Fenrir.

Whoever'd said silence was golden should have passed the memo along to his extended family. Fenrir, of course, had been delighted.

His device rang again. Niall scowled at it from across the room.

He was tempted to ignore the damn thing; only the thought that it could be Mat convinced him to answer. Rising from his seat, he stepped to the counter and snatched the phone up from where he'd tossed it earlier that morning.

It wasn't Mat.

Your Favorite Colleague flashed across the screen. Not *Mat.* Dammit, he still had to answer the damn thing. Ryder Mann had changed his name in Niall's phone months ago and Niall couldn't be bothered to change it back. Yet.

"What?" Niall growled into the handset.

"Cripes." Ryder sounded exasperated. "How many times do I have to tell you that *what* is not how to answer a phone call?"

"Fine, hang up and call back and I won't answer at all. My morning will go back to its regular programming." And he would return to his obsessive rehash of the J. Doe file.

What was he missing?

West Coast Forensics often worked cold cases without charge. All the investigators would sit around a table and pick a case to focus on until it was solved, or a year had passed and the team picked up another. With an estimated 40,000 unidentified deceased in the US alone, there were too many cases to choose from.

Over a year had passed since he'd chosen case JD107, but Niall wasn't finished with it yet. He felt a pull to this one and had the elusive feeling that the solution lingered just out of sight —like an itch in the middle of his back. He wanted to give the remains their identity back.

"Are you caffeine deprived?" Ryder demanded. "Do I need to drive some beans over?"

"Please, no."

Ryder Mann was a nice guy and a great coworker. And also married to Niall's half brother—how Shay stood all the talking, Niall had no idea. The guy had a mouth that never stopped. Maybe he was spiritually related to Alyson Dempsey, who could withstand Riley's chatter with no apparent problem.

"Why are you calling me?"

The weekly all-staff meeting wasn't for a few days yet, and he wasn't behind on anything. There had to be some other reason. Niall had a feeling he wasn't going to like it.

"Right. About that." Ryder's tone was serious now. "I just got off a call with a police detective from Barstow, California."

Barstow. One of Niall's least favorite places. He'd been there once for work and once because it existed between points A and B. The last time was a few years ago and the city hadn't improved since his first visit. Mostly, it had been hot.

"I'm not on call this month," he reminded Ryder. Unless there was an active case that demanded his area of expertise, he was staying on the island with Mat and Fenrir.

"Yes, Niall, I know this. She called us because there was a hit on some evidence they submitted to the NDIS a while back."

Niall could almost hear the eye roll Ryder was giving him.

The National DNA Index System was the Feds' best tool for identifying unknown persons. John Does, Jane Does, any Does out there. It wasn't perfect by any means, not even close—the system was slow and relied on volunteers and family members giving up DNA samples—but when it worked, it worked.

"One of my cases?" He racked his brain trying to think of which case might have been plugged into the database. He didn't think Tanya Nichols's DNA had been loaded up; after all, they knew her identity. And Niall knew who her killer was, but the creep had left no evidence. He didn't think his contact at Seattle PD had found anything new, but one of these days, Jeremy Vaughn would make a mistake. And Niall would cheer.

"Not exactly," Ryder said enigmatically.

"Dammit, Ryder, quit fucking around." The paperwork he was supposed to be going over for the Lindsey case, the official reason he got to stay on the island for a bit, was spread out across the kitchen table, and he needed to get back to it—as soon as he reread the Doe file.

The silence on the other end of the line made his eyelid

twitch; Ryder was always talkative. "Spit. It. Out. I don't have all day." He rubbed at his eye.

"Alright. So, ten years ago, unusually heavy spring rains caused some flooding in Barstow," Ryder spoke quickly. "A Department of Transportation worker was checking culverts and discovered human remains in one of them. Hands and feet were bound, no ID, no one had been reported missing recently. No one in the area seemed to know who the victim was, yada yada. Even though they had a sketch done and publicized the incident, no one came forward."

Niall leaned his hip against the counter. Fenrir, who'd been curled up on his massive dog bed, rose to his feet and padded across the room to nose Niall's hand. Hel, Fenrir's cat, followed after him and wound around Niall's ankles in a show of support. Or maybe she was just planning to trip Niall when he wasn't paying attention.

"Long story short, the coroner collected some samples and saved them. A few years ago, the sample was sent to a national lab when the county was awarded a grant to pay for DNA from cold cases, but there were no matches to the Jane Doe at the time. Barstow called us today because they recently received an alert that their sample matched closely with someone we have in our office. On our staff. That person is you."

Niall's stomach lurched.

Ryder's voice dropped as he continued speaking. "The possibility that the match is wrong is under one percent. This sample belonged to someone in your maternal line, someone very closely related to you. There's a fancy name for it but I doubt you want to know what it is. It's your mom, Niall."

The reassuring rasp of Fenrir's wiry coat against his fingertips kept Niall grounded. He was in his kitchen at his cabin. The scent of freshly brewed coffee was heavy in the air. Mat had left for work a couple of hours ago. Things were the same even though his world had just shifted in a yet-to-be-defined way.

Ana Hamarsson had been found.

A few months ago, Kimball and Leo—the owners and masterminds behind West Coast Forensics—had asked Niall to submit a DNA sample. This was common procedure, followed in case a field agent unintentionally, through injury or some other cause, contaminated a scene.

Niall had considered submitting his DNA in the past in the unlikely event his mother's remains turned up, but he'd never followed through. In truth, he'd been sure she was dead for years.

Sometime after Niall's seventh birthday, Ana Hamarsson had dropped off the end of the earth, so submitting DNA seemed pointless. It wouldn't change anything.

He dragged air into his lungs as he seemed to have forgotten to breathe for a few seconds, maybe minutes. Niall didn't know.

"You okay?" Ryder sounded worried.

Another deep breath, another nuzzle from Fenrir.

"Yeah, you just caught me off guard with that." As if news like this would ever catch a person *on guard*.

After all these years, Ana Hamarsson had finally turned up. Dead, as expected. He'd never entertained a different outcome for his mother. That she'd died violently was no surprise. Would he have preferred an alternative ending for her? Yes.

He shook his head, bemused. The brain was such a strange organ. Why was he abruptly melancholy even though he'd suspected the truth for the majority of his life? Why did the violent death of a woman who'd callously abandoned him— when he'd hardly been a boy—upset him now? Ana Hamarsson had made her choices and they'd never been good ones. It wasn't as if he ever thought she might be alive somewhere, just waiting to make amends.

Niall did not believe in amends.

"There's another thing," Ryder said cautiously.

Fuck.

Niall shut his eyes, blocking out the watery spring sunshine creeping in through the kitchen window. There was always another goddammed thing. Why couldn't life be simple?

"Your DNA wasn't the only hit they got."

He opened his eyes.

"I'm sorry, what?" He pinched the bridge of his nose.

"There's a second match," Ryder confirmed. "Detective Garcia didn't want to divulge the name, but I convinced her it was in her best interest."

Ryder would've hacked into their system if they refused. By sweet-talking the detective, WCF's computer expert didn't have to break the law. Really, he'd done them a favor.

Another relative? A long-lost cousin? The problem with that train of thought was that the Hamarsson tree was stunted. His grandparents had emigrated to the States sometime after 1945 and before 1960, and Ana had been their only child.

"What's the name?"

"Dakota Owen Green. I did some quick research. Twenty-four years old, last known address in Wyoming. Seems like he moved around a lot as a kid, but he was born in Barstow, California, so there's our legitimate connection. Interestingly," Ryder continued, "he fell off the radar sometime in the late 2000s, when he'd have barely been a teenager. Then he popped up again about six years ago. Now he's working at some hip brewery called Jake's Tap in Collier's Creek, Wyoming. Just graduated from the local community college, but he's been waiting tables for a while."

It was generally best not to ask how Ryder got his information. If Ryder couldn't figure out where Dakota Green had lived for almost a decade, the guy had to have been seriously off the grid.

"Keep talking." Ryder had paused for air, but Niall knew he had more to tell him.

"Because of the information you sent in with your DNA sample, the remains have been tentatively identified as those of Ana Green, formerly Ana Hamarsson. An Ana Green worked at a truck stop outside Barstow for a few months. I haven't found much more than that."

"There doesn't seem to be a point for you to look further. She's dead," Niall said with a bitterness that surprised him. "By the late 2000s, she'd been dead to me for twenty-five years."

Ryder paused, and when he spoke again, his tone was almost reproachful. "No one reported her missing—at least, not back then."

Niall glared out the window again. The tide was coming in, rolling against the rocky shore, pushing some driftwood up and back down the beach. Damn, he shouldn't be an asshole. Ryder's mom had disappeared too, and her body still hadn't been found.

A missing mother was something they had in common.

"Also not a surprise." He kept his tone neutral this time.

"Niall, you have a brother." Ryder sounded exasperated, as if he'd expected Niall to jump up and down with joy at the prospect of a new blood relation.

"A half brother," Niall corrected. "And I already have one of those."

Shay Delacombe—Ryder's husband and Niall's half brother—was a couple of years older than Niall. This meant Niall was also related to Claribel Delacombe, Piedras Island's matriarch and Shay's great-aunt. So yeah, he did have other relatives, just not on the Hamarsson side.

David Delacombe, Shay's morally questionable father, had

started an affair with Ana Hamarsson when she'd been under-age. Maybe he'd really cared for her? Maybe they'd cared for each other? It didn't matter. No one alive knew what the truth was because Shay's father had died years ago and Ana had fled the island before anyone had even suspected she was pregnant.

Ryder interrupted Niall's meandering thoughts. "What are you going to do?" His tone was soft. Niall appreciated the effort.

While Niall rarely talked about it, he'd given Shay permission to share their story with his husband. Shay's childhood had been diametrically different from Niall's, but they'd both suffered from the lies and the loss.

What he really wanted to do was ignore the whole fucking situation, but that, unfortunately, was not how his mind worked. He suspected Ryder would relentlessly pester him about why he wasn't following up on this information if he didn't do anything.

"I don't know, Ryder. I need some time to think."

Ryder didn't immediately respond. For a moment, Niall thought the call had dropped. He checked his screen; they were still connected.

"I can respect that," Ryder finally stated. "If it were my mom, and I found out there was a relative or sibling I hadn't known about, I don't know what I would do. All these years have passed and what if she'd left because she just didn't want to be my mom anymore? What if she started a new life some-where else?"

Niall opened his mouth to respond but Ryder got there first.

"Trust me, I don't believe that. Mom left the apartment with the intention of returning. I know in my heart that something terrible happened and she's dead. But sometimes, in the dark of night when I can't sleep, thoughts sneak up on me."

While Niall watched, a bigger wave thundered up the

beach and pushed the driftwood log far enough that it stayed above the tide line this time.

It was far too easy for Niall to relate to Ryder's thoughts. He'd been in foster care—Ryder had been lucky to live with a friend of his mother's—until Niall's grandparents learned he existed. Coming to Piedras was the second-best thing that had ever happened to him, but he still had emotional scars.

Mat Dempsey. The first best thing.

Niall still had violent nightmares. And Mat woke him up from them every time, even when Niall lashed out in his sleep, trying to escape the closet or the flames.

MAT

Something was bothering Niall.

Mat sensed it immediately after pushing through their front door. His husband wasn't the most demonstrative person, but he usually at least cracked a smile when Mat arrived home after being gone all day.

After several years together, Mat also knew that Niall would talk in his own time—for the most part—so he didn't ask him what was on his mind. Instead, he peeled off his jacket and toed off his boots before bestowing Fenrir the required scratch behind the ears while Hel wound around his ankles in an attempt to trip him up.

"Next time we have to rescue an idiot hiker from Dead Man's Bay, I'm considering ignoring the call," he stated. He, of course, wouldn't ignore a call, but the temptation was there.

Niall grunted. Mat assumed it was a *keep going* response.

"We are not a rescue agency."

The Piedras County Sheriff's Department, however, acted as backup for the Piedras Island Fire Department. Mat had rescued his fair share of kittens from trees and baby ducks from culverts since taking the sheriff's position.

"So why rescue them? Couldn't Flynn get down there?"

As the salaried head of the volunteer fire department, Devon Flynn probably had better things to do than save people from their own stupidity.

"Flynn was doing some educational thing with Jennings at the elementary school," Mat grumbled. "All the warning signs in the world and some gal still tried to do the trail by herself in the rain. She was stuck halfway up the bluff for *maybe* an hour. Frankly, I think she could've made it back on her own."

"I thought they'd closed that trail until June or something."

Niall finished chopping some green onions, pushed them aside, and began grating cheddar cheese.

"Yeah, well, she 'didn't see the notice.' Then we had to respond to a trespassing call from Sandy Johnson, and this time it wasn't just because she wanted some conversation."

Another grunt from Niall. He scooped up the cheese and tossed it into a small bowl that they'd brought back from their honeymoon in Thailand.

"Two photographers—and I use the term loosely—followed a pair of red foxes onto Sandy's property and wouldn't leave when she asked them to. So that was fun and I got to write my fourth trespassing warning of the year. I think March is going to break a record. What's cooking?"

He already knew it was chili; he'd smelled it when he came inside.

"Chili, cornbread, and your mom brought over cookies. Oh, and green salad."

Abandoning the head scratches—there would never be enough of them for Fenrir—Mat padded across the room to the round table they used both for meals and as an office when working from home. A plastic container he recognized as one of his mom's sat in the middle. Lifting the lid, he selected a cookie and took a big bite.

"Mmm. Chocolate chip, my favorite."

Mat'd had to up his daily runs to keep the sweets his mom and sister were constantly making from impacting his waistline, but after hiking down and back up Dead Man's Cliff in the rain, he deserved a damn cookie. Maybe two.

"I'm tempted to tell you not to ruin your dinner," Niall rumbled.

"Yeah," Mat said around another bite, "but I'm an adult and if I want a cookie before dinner, I can have one."

"Yep. One of the few great things about being an adult."

Fenrir sauntered over to stand next to him, resting his chin on the tabletop.

"No," Mat told the dog firmly. "You may not have a cookie. We all know that chocolate is bad for dogs."

"Is it though?" Niall said. "Or is it a devious human plot to keep all the best treats to ourselves?"

The look Fenrir shot Mat was scathing and filled with disgust. How a nonverbal beast was able to telegraph his thoughts and feelings so well was a constant source of amusement for Mat.

"No," he repeated.

Fenrir huffed, eyeing him as if he fully expected Mat to change his mind.

"Riley dropped off some treats for Fenrir and Hel earlier," Niall said, pointing the wooden spoon he held at a second plastic container sitting on the end of the counter.

"Oh, I see how it is. Bribery all around."

Grabbing the second box, Mat took out several of the home-made treats. Turning back around, he found Fenrir and Hel sitting on their haunches next to each other, looking as if butter wouldn't melt in their mouths.

"Were you good today?" Mat asked.

"If you call chasing each other around the yard through

every mud puddle they could find, good. Then, yes, they were good."

Mat still found it funny that Hel thought she was a dog. The young cat didn't act like a normal feline at all. She even swam in the chilly waters of the strait when she thought it was warm enough. They had several videos of her riding Fenrir in the waves like she was some kind of mer-cat.

Breaking the biscuit into pieces, Mat held out a chunk to Fenrir, who took it gently from between his fingers. Hel was not so careful. Mat set hers on the floor and then watched as they gobbled them down. Ten seconds later, they both looked expectantly at him for more.

"Maybe later."

With a snort of displeasure, Fenrir turned his back on Mat and clomped back to his dog bed, where he flopped down with a huff. Hel eyed Mat a moment longer before joining Fenrir on the bed. From there, they both glared at him. Mat shook his head and turned back to Niall.

"Ryder called with some interesting news." Niall was at the stove now, his back to Mat as he stirred his signature chili. "About Ana."

Mat sucked in a breath between his teeth. If Ryder Mann had called Niall, it meant something big had happened. Crossing his arms, Mat stepped to the counter and propped his hip against it so he could at least watch Niall's profile.

"What did he have to say?"

"You know that DNA I submitted a while back?"

Mat nodded. There'd been a lot of discussion in the Dempsey-Hamarsson household about Niall sending in a sample. In the end, Niall hadn't had a choice because WCF had required it. The decision was taken out of his hands.

"There was a hit," Niall continued. "Until ten years or so ago, Ana was alive and living in Barstow."

Nodding again, Mat thought very carefully about his response. This news had to have Niall all twisted up inside. His mother had been alive all this time—or at least until not too long ago. She'd just... abandoned her son and never looked back? She'd never even tried to communicate with her family? Mat realized he'd secretly harbored hope for a better result.

Both of them had believed Ana was already dead, so the fact she actually *was* dead wasn't the surprise. The fact that there'd been a hit on Niall's DNA sample meant she'd been in the system as a victim of a crime. Unfortunately, also not surprising.

It was that her death had occurred relatively recently that had Mat reeling. And, no doubt, Niall too.

"What do you need me to do? What do *you* need to do?"

Whatever Niall needed, Mat would be there for him. The question was—how much would Niall admit to needing?

Reaching across the counter, Niall grabbed a ladle from the metal utensil holder. Without immediately replying, he began spooning chili into bowls he had ready. When he was satisfied with the serving amount, he picked the bowls up and brought them to the table, setting them down in between the stacks of paperwork taking up the rest of the surface area, then he pulled out a chair and sat.

Following Niall's lead, Mat sat across from him. The dog and cat made themselves comfortable, scooting as close to the table as they were allowed and watching and waiting for tidbits to fall to the floor.

"I'm not sure," Niall finally admitted.

"What else did Ryder say?"

Mat did not doubt that Ryder had learned as much as he could about the test results before alerting Niall.

"Not much." Niall spooned chili into his mouth.

But there was something. Mat *knew* there was something else. Niall was working up himself to sharing whatever it was.

Again following his lead, Mat took a bite of the chili. As always, it was delicious. Spicy—but not too much— and with a deep flavor that Mat was never able to replicate when he did the cooking.

After swallowing, Mat asked, "But he found something?"

With a deep sigh, Niall set his spoon down and glanced up at the timber ceiling before looking directly at Mat for the first time that evening.

"Something, yeah. My sample wasn't the only hit. There's a boy. Ana had another son."

It was a good thing Mat hadn't taken another bite yet; otherwise, he would have choked on it.

"What the hell? You have a brother?" That Niall might have a long-lost relative had never crossed Mat's mind. Ana was an unfit mother the first time around. The idea of her having a second child was horrifying.

Niall's lips flattened into a thin line. "Another one? I guess so. Genetically anyway."

"She really had another kid?" Mat still was stuck on the reality that Ana Hamarsson had abandoned her first son and then gone on to have another one. What kind of life had he lived?

"Ryder got a name," Niall said.

"Of course he did."

Ryder was resourceful and savvy and no doubt he'd known what Niall would ask when he called.

"Name's Dakota Green. Twenty-four years old, lives in some town called Collier's Creek. In Wyoming."

"Wy-fucking-oming? How the hell did Ana end up there?"

Wyoming seemed about as far from Piedras as the moon, especially for what he knew of Ana. What had drawn her there?

"Ryder said he was born in California. Can't say if Ana made it as far as Wyoming. Maybe the kid moved there later."

California seemed much more likely a place Ana would have landed. If she'd hitchhiked, the I-5 corridor would be easy enough to take south, and Cali was the Golden State. Maybe she'd thought she could restart her life there.

"If he's twenty-four and she died a decade ago..." Mat let his voice trail off.

"He's been on his own for a while now."

Much like Niall. Albeit, older than Niall had been when Ana abandoned him. Mat wondered if that was worse or better as they ate in silence. By the time he was scraping the bottom of his bowl, he still didn't have an answer.

NIALL

That his mother might have been able to magically kick her drug habit and become a better person was a fantasy Niall had never allowed himself to indulge in. Not only had he been a part of too many drug-related homicide investigations to court that particular pipe dream, but he'd never counted on happy endings in the first place. He was amazed on a daily basis by the fact that somehow he'd managed to find one.

Definitely not because he'd been looking for it or because he deserved it. More like, happiness had found him and stuck, even though he'd tried to scare it away.

If Ana had once been a loving, caring person—drug use changed the kindest people *forever*. The Hollywood slash Hallmark happy endings were fairy tales written by people with no concept of reality. Mat had searched for Ana but never found a trace of her. Now they knew it was because she'd been long dead by the time he started looking.

"What are you thinking?" Mat prodded.

Mat understood him well. Sometimes it bugged Niall that he couldn't get away with his moods with his husband, but mostly he appreciated not having to explain shit all the time.

"This Dakota kid. Young adult, I guess. What is twenty-four counted as anyway? Do I reach out to him? Do I open this can of worms?"

What he wanted to do was finish going over the Doe file for the fiftieth time, but he hadn't been able to focus after Ryder's call. And he also had the Lindsay case—which Kimball Frye and Leo Zelinsky were actually paying him for.

Mat didn't answer right away, but Niall thought he recognized that silence. His husband was processing the information Niall had dumped on him.

Did he want to try and meet this... *kid*? Shit, he was young enough to be Niall's own son.

"Another child," Mat finally said. "Wow. What are you going to do? What do you want to do? And do you want me to come with you? To California, Wyoming, or both?"

Niall rolled his eyes. Was he just going to drop everything to sort out his mother's affairs? Did he want to meet with the homicide detective Ryder had talked to? She might ask hard questions, and Niall was used to being the one asking those.

"I don't know. You can't just leave the island, Mat. You know you can't," Niall said. "There's too much going on. With Radden on paternity leave for another week, you're even more short-staffed than usual. And don't try and tell me that Birdy can cover you because as efficient as she is, she's not actually Wonder Woman." Additionally, Niall had zero desire to listen to Leo Zelinsky bitch about his partner's evenings being taken up by more than her usual quota of teenaged vandals and jaywalkers.

"I don't think I like this." Setting his spoon in his bowl, Mat stood up from the table and carried both to the sink. Niall could tell from the set of his shoulders that he was holding back some strong feelings. Mat was a natural carer. It was what made him a great sheriff and partner. What he saw in Niall was somewhat of a mystery.

"Well, I don't know what I'm going to do, so don't lose any sleep just yet."

He gathered up his dinner dishes as well, setting them in the sink with Mat's and just barely missing Fenrir as he sidled across the room to see if any interesting bits had dropped to the floor. When he didn't find anything, he shot Niall a soulful glance.

"Let's go for a walk."

A stroll on the beach, even in the rain, would clear Niall's head a bit. He needed the fresh air after brooding a good part of the day.

Mat, being the good sport he was, readily agreed and within minutes, the four of them were heading down the pebble pathway to the beach. At the water's edge, Niall did as he always did and took a moment to offer thanks to his grandparents and whatever rogue spirits had ensured that he survived and made it to this place and time. To Mat.

Fenrir woofed and raced off to chase the waves that dared to trespass on his land. Hel was right by his side, doing her best to scare the water away with her creepy, cackling squawk.

He and Mat stood shoulder to shoulder, their hands jammed into the pockets of their coats. Mat was quiet, which Niall both appreciated and hated. But this was his decision to make, not Mat's or Ryder's or anyone else's but his.

Fenrir lunged and barked, the waves rolling in regardless of his complaints. Niall was reminded of the night a few years ago when he'd said his goodbyes to Ana. He'd launched a wooden boat across Haro Strait and watched as it burned to the waterline, releasing her spirit and his grief. Would bringing her remains back mean revisiting all that?

Likely.

But if he didn't, he'd just constantly think about what happened to her. About her bones in some anonymous grave. About the kid she'd had after Niall.

"I'm going to go to California," he announced. A bigger wave formed and both Fenrir and Hel backed away, letting it come ashore and wash away again.

"Okay. And what about Wyoming?" Mat asked.

Fucking Wyoming.

Niall had never been the type of person to shy away from responsibility. He'd go to Wyoming—to the tiny town of Collier's Creek—and he'd find this Dakota Owen Green. After meeting him, he supposed that Dakota's response to Niall's appearance in his life would be the deciding factor. Then he'd figure out his next steps.

He doubted the kid was any more aware of Niall's existence than Niall had been of him. But, for his grandparents, he would do the right thing.

"I don't like it," Mat grumbled.

"To be honest, I don't like it either," Niall said. "But it's the right choice. I'll fly down to Barstow, talk to this detective, and make arrangements for Ana's remains."

They continued to stand a while longer and stare out over the cold, gray water of the strait, watching the waves as the sunlight finally disappeared from the horizon and the wind picked up and brushed along the tops of the evergreens, causing them to sway along with the rolling swells of ominous, dark water.

Mat nudged Niall's shoulder. "Fine. It's the right thing to do. I'm freezing now, so let's wrangle the beasts and get back inside."

She'd been the shittiest of parents but Ana had been his mother, and his grandparents had loved their daughter even if they'd never understood her. Niall would honor them by not abandoning her in some anonymous plot in the desert. He'd bring her home to the island she never should have left.

The anger he'd held onto for decades had dissipated years ago, leaving mostly sorrow in its wake. At least he could help her remains find peace. Was he angry she'd had another son? He wasn't sure. He didn't think so. She hadn't been a great mom the first time around. Mostly it worried him that another human probably suffered because of Ana's choices.

"After Barstow, I'll fly out to Jackson. Or maybe I'll drive," Niall said while he toweled down Fenrir and Hel in the mudroom. Really, it was just an enclosed front porch area, but Alyson insisted on calling it a mudroom.

"What about your case?" Mat asked, hanging his coat up next to Niall's.

Dammit. Ryder's call had erased the upcoming Lindsay trial from Niall's mind. He eyed the paperwork stacked on the kitchen counter. He had at least two weeks before he needed to travel, maybe longer if it was delayed again. And the trial was being held in San Francisco, easy enough to get to at the last minute if need be.

"I have time, plenty of it."

"When are you planning on leaving?"

Niall opened his laptop and started scrolling through available flights. "I can get a flight midmorning tomorrow."

"I wish I could go with you," Mat said with a soft sigh.

Niall understood; if their roles had been reversed, he would have wanted to support Mat. But Mat carried the responsibility for the safety of Piedras Island, and the rest of the county, on his shoulders. Leaving Hidden Harbor at the last minute was not an option in the best of circumstances, but especially not with deputies on leave.

· · ·

LATER, long after dinner, after walking Fenrir and Hel to the beach and back, after his suitcase was packed, Mat made certain Niall would miss him. Or wouldn't—Niall wasn't sure which.

"What was that about?" Niall managed to rasp out when he could speak again.

"I don't like that you're doing this on your own."

"Feeling a little protective, are you?"

Niall got it, he felt the same way about Mat. And Mat was the one putting himself in harm's way every time he left the house.

Abruptly, Mat rolled on top of Niall again, crushing Niall into the mattress as he glowered down at him.

"Yes, I'm feeling fucking protective," Mat growled.

Niall loved it when Mat growled. Normally it was Niall doing the growling. A riled-up Mat Dempsey was unusual.

"Why? I go away on cases on a regular basis."

"Because this isn't just a case, and I worry you're going to get lost in your head without the voice of reason—that's me, by the way—to keep you on an even keel."

"I'll call."

"You bet your ass you will."

In the dim light of their bedroom, Mat's mouth found his again. Groaning, Niall opened up for him. He always would. Mat Dempsey was his safe place. Niall would miss his husband —Mat was the light to Niall's dark—but it couldn't be helped.

He would do this one last thing for his grandparents. Niall wouldn't let them down.

MAT

"Can you repeat that?" Mat asked the speaker, incredulity lacing his tone.

At the desk adjacent to his, Birdy stopped her fingers from flying over her keyboard to listen to Mat's side of the conversation. Normally, Birdy or one of the other deputies answered the public line. But, no, he'd gone off the plan and picked up the phone when it rang instead of heading to the break room like he'd meant to, and now he was regretting it. Not that ignoring the call would've changed the outcome. Someone on the midmorning sailing had died a violent death. And he still wouldn't have had a fresh cup of coffee.

Dammit.

He was off his game with Niall being gone. That was the only explanation for needing the caller to repeat themself.

Mat listened again to what the person on the other end of the line told him while he also stood up to start putting on his coat.

"There's a dead guy in one of the cars on the ferry. We looked through the window and"—the caller audibly swallowed—"we think he was shot."

"You're sure he's not breathing?"

"I think it would be impossible, Sheriff."

Catching Birdy's eye, Mat nodded. She rose to her feet as well and pulled on her PCSD jacket over her uniform.

"Okay, we'll be there ASAP. Three minutes, give or take. Try and make sure no one leaves the scene."

"This was the last car, sir. All the rest have disembarked."

Double dammit.

"Tell the captain the boat has to stay put until we're done investigating."

He didn't have to walk further than outside the building housing the Sheriff's Office to see that there was a line of cars idling—which was against city ordinance—on the street outside. He estimated around twenty vehicles were waiting to load onto the midmorning sailing.

"Yes, we've done that. People aren't going to be happy."

No, they wouldn't be, but they were just going to have to wait a little longer.

"You might want to call the state and have them send another ferry out. I'm short-staffed and we're going to need to search the entire boat."

"THE ONLY GOOD thing about this is that it's midweek," Birdy said, glancing from where they stood back out to the dock and the relatively short line of vehicles waiting to leave the island.

"Yep," Mat said glumly.

Collectively, he and Birdy returned their attention to the late model series BMW. A very dead person sat behind the steering wheel.

"No way would anyone have heard a gunshot over the ferry engines," Birdy commented.

"Nope," Mat agreed.

A deckhand—easily identifiable by the orange reflective vest he wore along with heavy work pants, boots, and a thick, waterproof jacket —stood nearby, nervously shifting on his feet. The deckhand had noticed the car still on the ferry after all the other cars had driven off and, he had told them, the doors had been locked.

"I knocked on the window to get his attention, like wake him up or something, and the driver didn't respond. I mean, obviously, he was dead, but I didn't know that. My first thought was that he'd had a heart attack or something, so I tried the door." He lifted his gloved hand. "That's when I noticed, um, the rest of him."

After gloving up, Mat and Birdy had managed to get the driver's side door open. The alarm blared but Mat disarmed it with the remote key sitting in the console. Once the alarm wasn't echoing off the interior of the ferry, he crouched down to get a better view of the body.

"White male. In his forties, I'd say. Gunshot wound to the temple."

It wasn't pretty, but scenes like this never were. But the head rest had taken the worst of it. Mat could see how it was possible the crew member hadn't been able to tell anything was wrong until he looked closer.

Birdy took down notes while Mat squinted into the gloom of the vehicle and rattled off what he saw. Unfortunately, he didn't see anything obvious—like a gun. Using his flashlight, he peered underneath the seat, between the seats, and into the back of the car. Nothing.

The car was spotless, except where the gore from the head wound had ended up along the back of the driver's seat and dripped a bit into the back of the car. It was one of those Hollywood myths that a bullet to the head would spray brain everywhere. It depended on angle, location, caliber of the weapon. A bunch of stuff that sometimes Mat wished he didn't have to know from personal experience.

There was also no car seat, so presumably the victim didn't have a small child waiting somewhere to be picked up. He straightened.

"There's no sign of a weapon in the car, so we're gonna need more bodies. Call Jones and Jorgensen to come help us search the boat."

While Birdy made the calls, Mat circled the car, checking for anything obvious: a bloody handprint, maybe a piece of fabric from someone's jacket, or, by some miracle, a gun sitting underneath the vehicle with a note from the driver explaining what had happened.

Although how a dead man would have gotten it there would've raised other questions.

Birdy followed after him, arriving just as he popped the back hatch and lifted it all the way open. They both glanced inside. It was as spotless as the rest of the vehicle. No murder weapon. He pulled up the protective mat. Nothing there, either, only the tools to change a flat tire.

"No bag," Birdy noted.

And no suitcase. That was interesting.

"Nope," Mat agreed. "I don't think I recognize him. Do you?"

"No, I don't. But he could be a newbie. Or he just travels light, a tourist visiting for the day."

Mat shut the hatch again and peeled off his gloves, stuffing them in his pocket to toss out back at the station.

"I'm just hoping islanders haven't resorted to murdering tourists before they arrive."

"So," Birdy said, frowning at his words, "someone shot our

guy and either took the weapon with them, hopped into their own car, and drove off, or tossed it into the strait and then still drove off?"

Now they both turned and looked out of the other end of the ferry, where the chilly water that made up Hidden Harbor churned under the ferry's idling engines. The whole setup would've led Mat to suspecting suicide had the gun not been missing, but Marshal would clear that up by testing for powder residue on the victim's hands.

"That's what *I* would do," Birdy continued. "The damn thing could be anywhere between Hidden Harbor and Anacortes."

Mat glanced around the ferry deck again. The crew was a small one, only ten people and that included the captain. It was March and, as Birdy had pointed out, midweek. This was probably the minimum number of workers it took for the ferry to leave the dock in Anacortes. Mat tried not to sigh too loudly. They needed to question every one of them before the ferry left Hidden Harbor.

"Call Don and get him and his tow truck down here. We need the car off this boat before we can think about releasing the ferry. While you're doing that, I'll take all the pictures of the scene I can think of. Also, get a hold of Marshal Soper and the Coast Guard. Bernard Viser and I will hash out later who's in charge of this mess. Hopefully, Soper can get out here ASAP." Another sigh escaped. "This is the most ridiculous crime scene I've ever tried to process," he complained.

"Agree, boss," Birdy replied, the snarky lift of one eyebrow reminding him that Birdy Flynn knew how to do her job. She didn't need Mat to tell her how to do it, unlike many of the other deputies.

"With any luck at all, the local Guard will take over the

case." Unfortunately, Mat had a bad feeling about what his luck might bring him. All the agencies were short-handed these days. He suspected that it would be a case of who'd gotten there first.

Which was the Piedras County Sheriff's Department, dammit.

APPROXIMATELY TWO HOURS and twenty minutes later, Tow Truck Don was following Marshal Soper's battered Land Rover toward Island Medical and Mat was giving the ferry's captain the all-clear to load up the next round of passengers and head for the mainland. There had been no alternate ferry, and Mat's deputies had been fielding increasingly aggressive questions from impatient drivers waiting to leave. Apparently, there was only so much time allowed for interviewing possible witnesses and doing everything else that needed to happen during a murder investigation.

Mat was feeling increasingly irritable.

Each of the crew interviews had followed the same script after they'd gathered personal information.

Job position on the ship? Captain, chief mate, quartermaster, bridge officer, chief engineer, deckhand/seaman.

What were you doing during the voyage? My job.

Where were you during the voyage? Engine room, wheelhouse, cafeteria, et cetera.

Were you acquainted with the deceased in any way? No.

Did you see the deceased at all during the voyage? No.

"Maybe Dr. Soper will find something when he examines the victim," Birdy said hopefully.

At least they were pretty sure they had the victim's name: Arsen Lloyd Hollis. Mat had gleaned that important bit of information from the title tucked into the BMW's glove compartment. He supposed the car could belong to someone else, that possibly the driver was not Arsen Hollis, but Mat doubted it. And anyway, a positive identification was Marshal's job.

"Do you want to head up to see Soper or go back to the office?" he asked Birdy.

"If you don't mind, I'll take the autopsy."

"Believe me, I've seen enough of those in my career. You're welcome to it."

There wasn't much call for autopsies on the island, but Mat had attended his fair share of them when he'd been a detective in San Francisco.

"All right. I'll let you know what Dr. Soper finds out."

She started walking across the car deck toward the dock.

Mat touched his forehead with his index and middle fingers. "I'll finish up here and meet you back at the station."

THE OFFICE WAS empty when Mat finally returned. And, shockingly, there were no blinking red lights on the landline indicating that someone had called with a non-emergency issue. If Niall wanted to talk, he'd call Mat's personal cell phone.

Hanging his coat on the back of his chair, Mat sat down at his desk again and began the task of learning more about their victim. Sometimes the research was the easy part and immediately led to the perpetrator. Sometimes, like today, there were no red flags. There was nothing to indicate someone had it in for Hollis.

Arsen Lloyd Hollis was an unusual enough name that he only found one, and he was the registered owner of a gray BMW iX. A total poser car in Mat's opinion, but he didn't get paid for opinions, he got paid to keep the community safe. And like it or not, his office was responsible for finding Hollis's killer. Bernard Viser owed him one after this.

While he had it on his mind, Mat sent in a request to the

state for the video of all the cars leaving the *Chelan* after it had docked. Then he clicked back over and began a deep dive into Arsen Hollis.

Hollis was—or had been—forty-five years old. His home address was listed in Olympia. A quick search of Thurston County records showed that he was the only owner/taxpayer listed on the deed for a fourth-floor condo with a view of Mount Rainier. He'd had to look the address up on Zillow to find that information out.

That didn't mean there wasn't someone to notify—Mat just needed to dig further. He was going to have to resort to social media. He was going to be glad when Deputy Radden got back; he actually seemed to enjoy the various platforms.

"Bingo!"

He should have gone there first because Arsen was clearly not shy. He had a personal profile with a business page connected to it that featured the real estate brokerage he'd owned and operated: Arsen Hollis Real Estate, Your Pass to a New Home.

"For fuck's sake," Mat muttered. "What was the guy doing up here?" Olympia was a long three-hour drive from Anacortes —on a good traffic day. There were days it could take over five hours to get to the state capitol. "Come on, what else do you have for me, Arsen?"

It didn't take long for Mat to ferret out that Arsen was, or had been, gay. At the very least, he seemed to date only men. His profile wasn't private, and the women pictured on his profile were beautiful and well-dressed but seemed plastic to Mat's practiced eye. The men too, but Arsen had his arms around a lot of them.

Mat scrolled back in time, searching for something that might spark a lead. As he did so, he jotted down the names of anyone who was tagged and looked like they may have been close to the victim. Who knew, maybe his murder could have been fueled by jealousy or maybe the guy had made promises he couldn't keep.

"No obvious family," Mat muttered. "At least, none he wanted to connect to on social media."

He called the number listed on Hollis's business page and was completely unsurprised when it went unanswered. There hadn't been a phone in the car or on the body. There was no way a real estate guy wouldn't have a cell phone. So where was it?

"Probably at the bottom of the harbor along with the murder weapon." Mat forced himself not to grind his molars. He didn't have time for a visit to the dentist.

The phone on his desk rang, and he answered it immediately. Anything to escape from Hollis's well-documented life. The guy seemed to eat out often and took pictures of everything. Why did anyone need to know Hollis had eaten Waygu steak? Who the heck cared?

"Dempsey," he said into the mic.

"Hey, sweet pea!" Alyson Dempsey gushed.

A law enforcement officer for over twenty years and his mom still called him sweet pea. Mat supposed there were worse nicknames.

"Hey, Mom, what's up?"

"You sound preoccupied so I'll make it quick. I just called to invite you and that husband of yours over for dinner tonight. Riley and Ella are going to Science Night at the school, and I'll be knocking around the house on my own. I feel the need to make lasagna."

Mat's stomach rumbled. His mom made the best lasagna on the planet, and he'd fight anyone who said otherwise. But he hadn't told her about Ana Hamarsson's remains being found and before he did that, he needed to talk to Niall.

"Hmm, can I give you a call back? We have a situation here and I need to talk to Niall."

"I heard about the body on the boat. Is that the situation?"

Mat bit back a groan as he clenched his jaw. He didn't want to know just how his mother had already heard about the body; it wasn't from Birdy, that's for sure. News traveled lightning fast in his small community.

"Yes, it is, and no, I can't tell you any more. As soon as I talk to Niall, I'll let you know about dinner."

"Mat." Allyson sounded offended. "I know you can't tell me anything. You forget I was a sheriff's spouse for years."

"Sorry, Mom. It's just been a day already."

"Love you, hon. Call me as soon as you talk to Niall."

Mat stared at the black phone for a moment before pulling his cell out of his pocket and dialing Niall's number. As he expected, the call went to voicemail.

"Er, give me a call when you have a minute. Mom invited us to dinner tonight. If I go over there, she's going to weasel everything out of me, and I want to make sure it's okay with you before telling her about Ana. I can probably make excuses for this evening, but you know how she is." He paused. "I love you, call when you can."

Over forty years old and his mother still had the ability to get information out of him without saying a word. Truly, it was embarrassing. It would actually be better if his sister and niece were there too. Riley could always be counted on for distraction.

Another thought struck him.

"Crap."

If his mother *already* knew about the body, did she know that Niall had left on the first ferry that morning? Lord, why was he even asking himself that question? Of course she did.

And he'd evaded committing to dinner—featuring his favorite meal—so she already knew something was up.

"Fuck."

"It's been a while," Birdy said from behind him, scaring him half to death. "Do we need to get the swear jar out again?"

NIALL

Niall caught the early flight out of Seattle with minutes to spare. The flight itself was uneventful if uncomfortable. Economy class was not designed for someone of his height. And the lack of privacy meant that, instead of getting work done, he sat there and stewed about Ana's fate. About the existence of Dakota Green.

Regardless of the California heat, he didn't take his coat off after exiting the plane or while waiting for his ride from the airport into town. From experience, he knew that he'd be freezing in the subarctic air-conditioning of the police station soon enough.

He'd expected the seventy-eight-degree temperature outside the Barstow airport, but it was still unpleasant. The mild climate of Piedras Island and the Pacific Northwest was what Niall preferred. It was only March, for fuck's sake; how did people live like this?

"This is where you want to go?" The ride-share driver asked, his tone dripping with skepticism. He probably didn't pick up many people whose first destination in town was the cop shop.

"Yes, thank you."

AS HE EXTRACTED himself from the back seat of the Prius, his joints popped from the cramped flight and the confines of the car.

"Fucking hell, I'm getting old."

Niall stretched and grabbed his roller bag from the back, then strode purposefully toward the entrance of the station. Upon pulling the door open, he was met with a blast of freezing air that caused goose bumps to rise on his skin almost immediately. Sometimes he hated being right.

"May I help you?" asked the young cop who'd pulled the short stick and been assigned front desk duty for the day.

"I'm here to see Detective Garcia. She's expecting me."

The kid started typing something on the keyboard in front of him but before he could hit Send—or whatever he'd been planning—a door on Niall's left opened and someone waved him into the bullpen.

"Mr. Hamarsson? I'm Detective Garcia. Thank you for flying all this way on short notice. Or should I call you Detective as well?"

She'd done her research in the past twenty-four or so hours. Good.

"Niall is fine." Mr. Hamarsson was possibly his grandfather although Niall didn't know of anyone who'd called him that. And he'd left the title Detective behind when he left Seattle.

"I'm over there." Garcia pointed toward a desk crammed into a corner. "Have a seat. I did a little research once we found out you were coming. West Coast Forensics is a great outfit."

The partitions of the detective's cubicle were covered with handwritten notes, printed-out calendars, receipts, and, in one spot, several photographs of smiling kids.

"My nieces. I like kids," she added as she sat down, "but I also like giving them back at the end of the day."

Nodding, Niall took the chair at the side of her desk. He liked Mat's niece and Marshal Soper's stepson, Caleb. And by "liked," he meant watching them from afar. Kids scared the shit out of him.

"I assumed you wanted to look at the files. They're thin," she warned, pushing a manila file across the desk. "This happened before my time and the responding detective retired not long afterward." Pausing, she eyed him. "Not that I think Black skimped on the investigation, it just doesn't appear there was much to go on from the get-go."

The meager sheaf of papers had been stuffed into an anonymous manila folder. Niall laid his palm on top of it as if he could absorb the information by osmosis instead of opening the file and reading the words inside with his eyes.

Ana had lived for over two decades after the last time he'd seen her. This folder held all there was to know about Ana Hamarsson since the late 1980s. Everything about her reduced to measurable statistics.

"I printed it out for you to read through." Garcia held his gaze. "I kind of figured you'd want to know the details. Cops usually do."

"Thanks," Niall said as he picked up the file. "Is there a place I won't be in the way?"

Garcia snorted. "This is as good a spot as any in the building. Unless you want one of the interview rooms?"

"No, I've had enough of those for a lifetime."

"I'll leave you to it then," she said, rising to her feet again. "I'm going to grab a cup of coffee. Would you like one?"

"No, thanks. I don't miss cop coffee."

. . .

THIRTY MINUTES LATER, Niall had finished reading through the former Jane Doe file—twice. Garcia was right, there wasn't much.

Ana's remains had been found by a Department of Transportation worker sent out to check on the flooding Ryder had mentioned. The responding investigator, Detective Abe Black, had noted that, in his opinion, the victim had been killed somewhere else and dumped inside the culvert. Gritty crime scene photos clearly showed her hands and feet wrapped with what looked like nylon rope.

The kind of shit a person could buy anywhere.

Her face really wasn't recognizable, and Niall suspected that, by the time she'd been found, Ana's fingers and toes had been nibbled on by various creatures, making fingerprinting impossible. The artist's sketch bore some resemblance to Ana, but not much.

Detective Black had believed Ana had been there for several days, maybe even weeks, but the rain and flooding made the time of death difficult to pin down. The medical examiner had agreed with Black. After no one had reported any person of Ana's description missing in the area, the medical examiner had packed the DNA into cold storage, hoping someday they would learn something, and the case was officially labeled cold.

This wasn't unusual. In fact, this was how most evidence from cold cases was handled. Black had done everything right.

The autopsy at the time had revealed that Ana's hyoid bone had been crushed. She'd likely been strangled and thrown away. For ten years, until the DNA match had finally come through, Ana had just been another Jane Doe. Anger simmered in Niall's gut; no one deserved this fate, not even Ana Hamarsson.

Niall flipped the file closed. He'd read everything included in it a third time, then he'd used his phone's camera to take pictures of the printed pages so he could go over them again if he wanted to. He had a feeling the information would lead nowhere. It had been too long and there had been—as far as the coroner back then knew—no other DNA evidence.

Before leaving the station, he sought out Detective Garcia again.

"I left the file on your desk."

"Thanks."

"Were you able to notify the other relation?"

He was curious to know whether Garcia had talked to Dakota Green and if so, what her impression was.

She shook her head. "We only have an email as a point of contact. I put a call into the Collier's Creek Sheriff's Department, but I have a feeling it's pretty low priority."

Niall imagined it was. In his old life, he would have been pissed off, but being married to a sheriff with a small and over-worked staff meant he had more sympathy these days.

"I'm going to head that way and see what I can find," he informed Garcia.

"Thought so."

"Why?"

"If it were me learning I had a relative I hadn't known about, you bet your ass I'd want to meet them in person. Well," she amended, "after doing a background check anyway."

"Are you okay with me doing the notification? I don't want to step on too many toes."

Garcia laughed. "After reading up on you, I am one hundred percent sure you don't care whose toes you step on. But no, we don't have a problem with you doing the hard work. I wish you the best of luck." Her expression sobered. "I am sorry for your loss."

Niall didn't know how to respond and settled with, "Thank you." As an afterthought, he asked, "The detective, Abe Black, is he still in the area? I wouldn't mind talking to him and seeing if he has any more thoughts."

In Niall's experience, detectives often had a case—or more—that haunted them. God knew he did. And once they were retired, they tended to roll ideas around in their heads, maybe think of the case from a different angle.

"I don't know," Garcia replied, "but I can ask around."

"I'd appreciate it. If you talk to him, please give him my cell phone number."

"Will do."

Niall held out his hand and Garcia shook it. "I hope you find out what happened to her." She took her hand back. "You might not like what you find though."

"Oh," Niall said as he grabbed the handle of his bag, "I doubt I will like it. Ana didn't live a tidy life. Thanks again."

NIALL'S PHONE vibrated against his hip but he wasn't ready to talk to anyone yet, not even Mat. He left it in his pocket. Seeing the crime scene photos of Ana had been hard, harder than he'd thought it would be, regardless that he'd been seven years old and it had been decades since the last time he'd seen her. He needed more time to process before talking to anyone— even those he considered family.

"Christ, Alyson would be having a field day with this," he grumbled, turning randomly to the left. He started down the sidewalk, rolling his bag behind him.

He needed a rental car.

Or he could fly.

He stopped walking and looked around. What was he doing walking in this heathen weather? Across the street, Niall spotted the ubiquitous Seattle-based coffee chain. At least he knew what he was getting into and they had free Wi-Fi.

Inside, the store was colder than the police station had been. Was it a city ordinance that people had to freeze while working or enjoying a snack?

"A large black coffee."

"Um." The kid eyed Niall but seemed to realize that there was no need to ask him any further questions.

Niall tapped his card against the reader and had the molten coffee in his hand within seconds. Making his way to an empty table next to one of the windows, he set his things down, then took a hesitant sip of his drink and scalded his tongue. Maybe the reason they kept it so chilly was to cool down the damn coffee.

Setting the coffee aside for the moment, he settled in and pulled out his phone to check the screen. Mat had called. Niall knew Mat was worried and wanted to know how he was doing. Niall didn't have the answer to that question so he skipped listening to the voicemail. When he had a flight to Jackson Hole —that was the closest airport—and a rental car to get him to Collier's Creek, he'd call Mat back.

Besides, wasn't Mat supposed to be sheriffing? They hardly ever talked during the workdays. Niall never knew whether Mat was in the office or out reassuring Mrs. Johnson that the sound she'd heard was just a branch falling to the ground. And getting tea and a brownie in return.

No, he wasn't calling back now. He'd wait until he was somewhere more private and had more information to share with his husband.

Yes, that's what he would do.

Even though he generally hated it, today Niall was thankful for the high-end cell phone WCF provided. Tapping into Chrome, he keyed in "flights to Jackson" and began scrolling.

"Jesus Christ, I'm not made of money," he grumbled. But quietly, so no one around him could hear.

While he searched for an airline ticket that wouldn't put him into debt for the rest of his life, Niall sipped the hot coffee and vaguely acknowledged the terrible covers of '80s and '90s music that were playing overhead. When he started humming *Smells Like Teen Spirit*, he knew it was time to head out.

Mat hadn't called again and Niall squashed the amorphous feeling of guilt swirling in his stomach for not wanting to talk yet. They were both adults, after all.

MAT

Niall still hadn't returned his phone call, but Mat put his concern for Niall on simmer for the time being. Niall would call back tonight, he reassured himself. Meanwhile, Mat had other things to worry about. He forced himself to focus on Arsen Hollis.

"Anything interesting?" he asked Birdy when she returned from the hospital.

His head deputy nodded. "Yes, but there are still questions. The cause of death was confirmed as a gunshot wound to the temple."

"No surprise there."

"There was one thing." Taking her coat off, she hung it on the back of her chair but didn't sit down right away. "A big thing."

"Yeah?"

"There was significant powder residue on his left hand."

Mat thought back to the well-dressed man found dead in the front of a fancy BMW and shook his head.

"He shot himself?"

That wasn't surprising considering the scene, and if it wasn't for the fact that the car had been locked and there was no weapon, Mat would've been stamping the file with Closed.

"Okaaay. So where does that leave us? There had to have been someone else in the car with him. He didn't shoot himself, get up and toss the gun, then return and lock himself inside the vehicle."

"Dr. Soper said the residue was fresh."

"So he hadn't been skeet shooting or something? Practicing at the range?"

Mat knew that wasn't how it worked. Although it would be helpful to locate the gun that was used, for comparison.

"I don't know, I didn't ask Dr. Soper."

Mat seriously doubted the residue on Hollis's hand came from something other than the weapon that had killed him. For one thing, there'd been no Facebook pictures of him at a range, holding a weapon, or anything else along those lines.

"Check and see if he had a permit to carry. If we know what kind of gun we're looking for, that would be helpful."

Birdy sat down, tapped her keyboard, and began typing.

"Alright then, we have a suspected suicide." Mat leaned back in his chair, flipping a pen between his fingers while he considered Birdy's information. "I haven't learned much. Left a message on the number for his brokerage, but I have a feeling the message went to his damn missing phone." He sat forward again, setting the pen down. "His social media is about what I expected."

He had the website up still. Hollis was smiling at Mat from the screen. To Mat, the smile seemed fake, but did that mean anything? Maybe it was just Mat's knee-jerk reaction from growing up with a wheeling and dealing older brother who also sold real estate and turned out to be a bad person.

Stopping her gun permit search for the moment, Birdy

moved over to perch on the edge of Mat's desk so she could see his screen better.

"Hm, looks like he got out a lot. Liked good food," she remarked.

One of the more recent pictures had been taken at either a sushi restaurant or a place that served sushi. The biggest clue was a picture of his plate and another of him smiling and raising a glass of white wine, a fish tank behind him. Someone was leaning in from Hollis's left, but the photo had been artfully cropped so all they could see was dark hair and a cheekbone.

"I know I'm in the minority because even Niall loves it, but I do not think of raw fish as good food."

He kept staring at the screen. It would make sense that the other person was male, but the way the shot was clipped they could just as easily have been a woman. He kept scrolling, the photographic evidence of Hollis's life rolling past like a slide show.

Leaning in, Birdy poked at the desktop.

"He seems to go to this place a lot. We can call down to Olympia, find out if they knew him or the folks who showed up with him on a regular basis."

"Good thinking. Did Marshal find a wallet?"

Rising to her feet, Birdy shook her head. "Nope, no wallet."

"That's just plain weird. If the vehicle hadn't been left on the ferry, I'd say this was possibly a robbery gone wrong."

"All robberies are wrong, sir."

"Yes, but you know what I mean. Did our guy pick the wrong partner? What happened between Anacortes and here? Did the car board the ferry in Anacortes, or did it come on at Orcas?"

The ferries didn't always stop at every island. In fact, with the current boat shortage, a few islands only had two sailings on any given day. Anymore, there were no guarantees when it came to the ferry system.

Birdy moved back to sit in her chair, automatically reaching for her computer mouse and waking up her desktop again.

"I'll look at the schedule."

"When we get the surveillance video from the state, we'll know more."

Birdy wrinkled her nose. "That's going to take ages, sir. They're worse than cell phone companies when it comes to releasing information."

"You're telling me," Mat groused. They were trying to find a murderer and everyone—literally *everyone*—knew the first twenty-four hours were the most important. Yet the information they needed was too often throttled by the tentacles of bureaucracy.

"Too bad Ryder doesn't work for us."

Mat managed to suppress a chuckle; even Birdy couldn't bring herself to address Ryder as Mr. Mann. He was now married to Shay Delacombe but had elected to keep his last name. Which was good—there were enough Delacombes running around.

"Agreed. We're going to have to wait and see what the 'proper channels' decide to release to us. Where's the car now?"

"At the towing yard, locked in the back."

Mat rose to his feet.

"How about we head over and see if the Beemer has any more information for us? There's nothing like a good crime scene investigation to distract a person."

"What do you need distracting from, sir?" Birdy asked as she stood up again.

Mat had an *oh, crap* moment as he tried to figure out how to respond. He wished Niall would call back so he knew what to do. Was Niall okay with Mat sharing what he'd found out with Alyson? With Birdy, who is practically Mat's work-spouse?

He settled for, "Nothing I can really talk about at the moment."

"Okay, sir. Is it safe to assume that it has something to do with Hamarsson catching the first ferry this morning?"

Damn small town. Small island.

"Yes," he allowed. "Was I ridiculous in thinking no one noticed?"

"Yes, sir. You were."

THE CAR GAVE UP NOTHING. It was the most boring and expensive car Mat had ever attempted to extract evidence from.

Backing out of the front, Mat straightened to his full height.

"Did the man get his car detailed weekly or something?" Mat complained.

There was literally nothing for them to find. No trash, not even a gum wrapper or ChapStick tube. The man didn't have an empty energy drink can hidden in the depths, or a napkin tucked in between the seats. Even the spaces underneath them were clean.

"It's possible, sir. Maybe he used this vehicle to show potential customers around?"

"I suppose," Mat agreed while trying not to be irritated that the man hadn't been a slob. "Where was he headed on the island? Surely he didn't drive up from Olympia for a day trip. He was planning on staying somewhere, and I want to know where that somewhere was."

"Obviously, we're going to have to find someone who knew him in order to find that out."

Mat glanced over at Birdy. A smile twitched on her lips.

"Thanks for that, Deputy." He glanced at his watch and saw

it was almost six. Fenrir and Hel would be impatiently awaiting their dinner. "I'm heading home for now. Maybe by tomorrow, someone will have called us back."

"Maybe the state will have released the video by then too." Birdy's voice held more hope than it should've.

"When pigs fly, my friend, when pigs fly. Say hi to Leo for me."

Birdy shot him a semi-shy smile at the mention of her partner. Mat winked and she returned a full-on blush. There weren't many things that flustered Birdy Flynn, and Mat wasn't above some gentle teasing of his nearly unflappable deputy.

NIALL

Niall caught an evening flight to Wyoming, planning to rent a car at the airport and drive to Collier's Creek the next day. Jackson, thankfully, wouldn't be uncomfortably warm.

After the relatively short flight—again short enough not to be able to work on the WCF Doe file—Niall headed toward the rentals. He automatically chose the company with the shortest line, a habit that drove Mat crazy, and half an hour later, he was heading into the small city.

During the flight, he'd looked over what he'd photographed in Barstow, again, and gleaned nothing new. There was almost no information—just the crime scene photos, the autopsy report, and the statement from the Caltrans worker, Jack Wilson.

While waiting in line for a car, he sent the files over to Ryder, figuring maybe he'd see something Niall didn't. Probably by morning, Ryder would have learned everything there was to know about Jack Wilson and Detective Abe Black.

By the time Niall checked in at the hotel, a four-story rustic structure called The Lodge, and found his room on the third floor, it was past nine. As he pushed open the door to his room, he realized that after a restless night's sleep and running on adrenaline all day, he was tired, both physically and mentally.

Flicking the overhead light on, he plopped his roller case on the baggage rack and hung his computer bag on the back of the single chair provided. The curtains were slightly open to a view of a hill across the street, and he could just make out what appeared to be a ski lift, although it wasn't running.

While he was standing there trying to figure out why a ski lift would be in the middle of town, his cell phone vibrated in his back pocket.

The call was from Mat, he knew—because of course it was.

"Hey," Niall said.

"Hey back. How's it going in Cowboy Town?"

On his way back to the Barstow airport, Niall had texted Mat to let him know his next stop was Jackson. Mat hadn't responded, but Niall figured he'd been caught up in something sheriff-related.

"Fine. Anywhere is better than Barstow. Gotta say, though, I haven't seen any cowboys."

He hadn't been down to the bar yet though. He figured that was where he'd most likely spot them—or, at least, cowboy wannabes.

"I don't care about cowboys. I want to know how it went in Barstow."

"About as expected. There's not much to go on. File's about twenty pages front and back. I made arrangements for Ana's remains to be shipped home."

Exactly what he was going to do when she got there, Niall wasn't sure. He didn't know what Ana had liked, or how she had lived. But the few pictures he had of her smiling were on or near the water, so that was where he'd probably start.

Should he invite Dakota Green? Would he want to come to the far northwest corner of Washington State? Did he even know about where Ana had spent the first seventeen years of her life? It occurred to him that maybe his newly found half brother had more of a claim on Ana than he did.

He was still bringing her home.

"Good, good. I think there are a few people on the island who wouldn't mind saying a proper goodbye. Have you figured out how to approach Green?"

Turning from the window, Niall sat down on the edge of the bed, the mattress sinking a little under his weight. Usually, he liked that Mat knew what was on his mind—it meant he didn't have to explain himself all the damn time. Sometimes though, like these moments when he didn't know up from down, it was unnerving.

"Not really. I don't have a home address or phone number. Guess I'll have to stake out the place where he works. That's on my list for tomorrow."

"Niall," Mat said, his voice oozing patience. "This is not a stakeout. Dakota Green is not a criminal—well, as far as we know. Don't go in there as Detective Niall Hamarsson, ready to interrogate him. Just"—he paused—"be yourself." Niall snorted and on the other end of the line, Mat laughed too. "Okay, whatever. So maybe be yourself but seriously, try not to scare him."

"I'll do my best."

"I miss you," Mat said. "Um—" he began but cut himself off.

"What?"

"Nothing really, just worried about you. Mom invited us to dinner tonight."

"What did she make?" Niall's stomach growled. He loved Alyson's cooking. It was even worth discussing whatever book Riley was currently reading or the win-loss status of the island soccer team she played on.

"I didn't go. Because if I had, I would have ended up telling her about Ana's remains and your trip, and I wanted to make sure that's okay with you first."

Niall thought back to his early morning commute from Hidden Harbor to Anacortes. At zero-dark-thirty, the coffee shop had been open and he'd said hi to Stu Dennis and nodded to Teagan Morrison, who'd barely acknowledged his greeting. Niall liked Teagan. He wished there were more uncommunicative hermits like him on the island. He was positive Teagan hadn't run home and told his partner that he'd seen Niall getting on the early ferry.

"Well, I saw Stu Dennis this morning while I was waiting for the ferry, so the whole island probably knows I'm gone."

"Yeah, but they don't know why."

Niall's heart—which he'd hardly acknowledged for most of his life—did a little flip. Mat was always watching out for him and Niall still wasn't used to it.

"I miss you too. Go ahead and let Alyson know. It's fine, I guess. I'll be talking with Sage soon, too." Sage would help him plan the memorial and news would get around fast after that.

Mat huffed a little laugh. "'Fine, I guess' is pretty strong coming from you. I'll take an ad out in the Island Times."

"Fuck off," Niall said in the most loving of tones.

"Come home soon," Mat said before clicking off.

Niall's sleep was restless again that night, his subconscious troubled by old ghosts and spirits he hadn't met yet, and Mat wasn't there to remind him that none of them were real. Around three a.m. he finally fell into a dreamless sleep, waking up just after seven in desperate need of coffee.

One hour, several large cups of coffee, and a long conversation with Sage later, and Niall was back on the road.

. . .

COLLIER'S CREEK SEEMED like an alright little town. It was what Niall had imagined a typical western town looked like before he'd seen one in person. Wide streets with angle parking and lots of one- and two-story brick buildings that were home to residents and small businesses. He passed the Collier Creek Bed and Breakfast, which looked like it might be a decent place to stay for a few nights, and made a mental note to swing back around later.

A few blocks later, he passed the Wagon Wheel, which was the kind of place Ryder would insist on staying just for the horror of it. Niall crossed it off his list of possibilities.

Jake's Tap—apparently named after Jacob Collier, the town's founder—opened for lunch and stayed that way until late evening, every day of the week. Since he had no idea what days or hours Dakota Green worked, Niall planned on stopping in and asking the staff. With any luck, he'd be there today and Niall could be done with it.

As luck would have it, a beat-up pickup truck backed out of a space almost right in front of the pub just as Niall spotted their sign.

"Might as well get this over with," Niall muttered, pulling into the vacant spot.

After spending almost two decades in law enforcement and currently being involved in the private LEO sector, Niall looked like a cop. He probably smelled and tasted like one too. No matter if he wore jeans and a ratty sweatshirt or slacks and a blazer, he still looked like a damn cop. Today he'd dressed casually, hoping to at least seem like a cop on vacation.

Not that he'd ever taken a vacation. Not until he'd quit the force entirely.

The interior of the pub leaned hard into Collier Creek's Old West history. Not really a surprise, Niall supposed as he glanced around. Black vinyl-covered booths sat against the walls with tables arranged in the center, and a long, curved, dark wood bar took up the back and butted up against a kitchen door. Custom tap handles and bottles of liquor were reflected in the long mirror behind the bar, another holdover from the days of the Old West, when a man sitting and having a quiet drink wanted to be alerted to anyone sneaking up on him. Niall could relate.

He'd hoped to see a host stand so he could ask a few questions anonymously. Instead, the bartender called out a cheery "anywhere you like" from across the room as Niall let the door close behind him. The hope of quietly speaking with a chatty host-person was dashed.

The bar had several open spots. Niall chose one at the end and perused the beer menu while waiting for the bartender to come over and ask what he wanted.

"What can I get you?" The kid seemed to do a quick double-take before grinning at Niall as he stood in front of him, something he wasn't used to. Most people who didn't know him steered clear. Maybe it was his new deodorant. Maybe this kid—*young adult*—was as unflappable as Birdy Flynn.

"I'll try the Highway Man," Niall said. The name amused him. Plus, it was listed as light and he didn't want a heavy beer.

"Coming right up," Mr. Friendly said. Spinning around, he grabbed a glass, held it over the glass washer and then underneath the tap, then flicked the handle with the same hand holding the glass. All very suave and hip.

The guy looked to be in his twenties—what did Niall know about age these days anyway?—and wasn't wearing a name tag. Could he be Dakota? Niall appreciated not advertising your name to the world, but it would have come in handy in this case.

"Anything else?" Mr. Friendly wanted to know after setting Niall's beer in front of him. "The chili's great today."

"Sure, I'll have a bowl of chili."

"Cornbread?"

"Why not."

Friendly started to turn away, but Niall raised a hand to stop him.

"Does Dakota Green work today?" he asked.

Cocking his head to one side, Mr. Friendly eyed Niall with a little suspicion this time. He clearly wondered why Niall wanted to know his coworker's schedule and Niall had to appreciate his hesitance. "Lemme see. I'll have to check the schedule."

So at least that information was correct; Dakota still worked here. And the bartender wasn't him—unless he was a very good actor.

"Thanks, I appreciate it."

The pessimist in Niall—which would be most of him—figured Mr. Friendly was going to give Dakota the heads-up that someone was looking for him. Thus, he was pleasantly surprised when he returned a few minutes later with chili and information.

"It looks like Dakota is scheduled to be on at four." Mr. Friendly put down the bowl and held out his hand. "My name's Tad."

Niall reached across the bar. "Niall Hamarsson."

"Nice to meet you, Niall Hamarsson. Flag me down if you need anything else."

MAT

Mat was grouchy and out of sorts. He didn't like sleeping without Niall next to him in their bed.

Truthfully, he'd hardly slept at all, not falling into a deeper slumber until Fenrir finally climbed up onto the mattress and tucked in behind his knees. The wolfhound mix technically wasn't supposed to sleep on their bed, but Niall being away was a special circumstance.

Now Mat was awake and moving around far earlier than he liked. Arsen Hollis had crept into his dreams, keeping him distracted from the lack of Niall. Would they learn anything today that would point them toward his killer?

"Damn, I hope so," Mat said to the cat as he shrugged into his work shirt. Having nothing to go on was not where Mat wanted to be.

From her perch on the counter, Hel did not respond.

"You're not supposed to be up there," Mat informed her. As if the cat wasn't fully aware of her transgression.

The tiny beast did not move. She didn't even flinch as Mat moved toward the counter and their fancy coffee machine.

"I suppose you two want breakfast and outside time before I go to work."

He glanced at the clock on the stove. It wasn't so early that his mom wouldn't be awake. While he waited for the coffee to brew, he opened the door so the cat and dog could go do their business. He knew better than to feed them first; they'd never come back inside. He also pulled out his cell phone and called Alyson, who answered almost right away.

"Good morning, hun. Is everything all right? You never call this early."

"Yes, Mom, everything is all right," Mat assured her. "I just want to tell you something and then ask a favor."

"You know I'll do whatever is in my ability."

"Maybe sit down for a bit," Mat said. He then started relaying what they knew so far about the DNA match and everything else concerning Ana, which wasn't much. "And there's the case here too. I have a feeling I am going to be busier than usual today. Do you think you can come and check on Fenrir and Hel, maybe around noon?"

Noon would give Mat a little leeway before they decided to take matters into their own paws. He counted himself very lucky the two hadn't gotten into trouble the day before.

"How about you drop them off here," his mom suggested, "and then I can feed you later tonight when you're ready to go home?"

Mat released a sigh of relief. He hated worrying about the Terrible Two when they were left to their own devices. Fenrir wasn't as much of a rascal as he'd been when he was a puppy, but Hel could pretty much get into anything.

"That'd be great, thank you so much. Niall thanks you too."

"How is he doing with all of this?"

"One sec." Holding the phone to his chest, Mat opened the door to call for the dog and cat. He felt himself smile when he found them waiting there facing the door, the picture of innocence and good behavior. "Get inside, you two."

"Okay, sorry about that." With the phone tucked between his shoulder and ear, Mat talked to his mom while he scooped out the special homemade pet food Niall made. Damn spoiled animals. "To be honest, I'm not sure how he's doing. We didn't have much time to talk about it and he's hard to read over the phone. He sounded okay, maybe tired. There's another thing too."

"What's that?" Alyson's voice was full of concern. She probably had instantly decided one of them was terminally ill.

"Don't worry, it's not about Niall or me. There was more than one match for the DNA. It looks like Ana had another child. A boy."

"Oh my god," his mom breathed. "That poor child, what has he gone through?"

Trust his mother to immediately worry about someone she'd never met.

"Ryder did some research for Niall but didn't find much information about him at all. We know his name is Dakota Green, he's twenty-four, and he lives in some tiny town in Wyoming called Collier's Creek."

"Is Niall thinking about reaching out to him?"

"More than that. He's headed there now to see if he can find him. Like I said, there's not much to go on. He seems to have fallen off the radar a while back and then reappeared a few years ago. It's not a priority for the Collier's Creek Sheriff's Department to track the kid down and Niall wants to do it himself. I'm sure they're nice people and all, but they're a small outfit, just like here."

Alyson was quiet for a bit longer than Mat was comfortable with. It meant his mom was plotting.

"Mom," he said warningly, "whatever you're thinking, just *no*."

"I'm thinking," she began fiercely, "that no matter how horrible Niall had it—and you and I both know it was goddamned awful. Ana Hamarsson was, if not purposefully abusive, then guilty of neglect so terrible it *was* abuse. But Niall was a young boy when that happened and his grandfather brought him home. And it took Niall a long time to start healing."

"Yes, Mom, I do know this seeing as how I'm married to him. Voted Grumpiest Man on Piedras for several years in a row." Stu Dennis made a point of announcing it at the Farm-Stock Festival every year. Mat had to admit it was pretty funny and even Niall seemed to find the kudos amusing.

"Oh, the grumpy part is Niall's natural personality, I think. He took after his grandfather," Alyson said with a laugh. "Jo was the more outgoing one, for sure. What I'm getting to is this boy, this young man, had nothing. Ana robbed him of his chance to know his grandparents and his Piedras family. Who knows how he grew up? He may reject Niall and be angry. What if he was in foster care all this time? What if he had to live on the streets at some point?"

Most people would stop Alyson now and tell her she was being dramatic, but she was one of the few people who knew the full extent of Niall's history. He had been in foster care for a short time and likely hadn't ended up on the streets only because of his age when Ana disappeared and the kindness of the police officer who'd found him.

"I don't think he's on the streets now, but I see what you mean. I guess we'll have to cross that bridge at some point."

"I know Niall is an adult and a smart person. I just don't want him hurt if this Dakota Green tells him he doesn't want to have a relationship."

It was Mat who laughed this time. "Honestly, I don't think Niall will be that hurt if that happens. This is purely him doing the right thing."

"I hope so." Alyson didn't sound quite convinced.

Mat looked at the clock again and groaned internally. He needed to get to work. "Crap, I've got to go. I'll be right over with your grandpets."

He poured himself a to-go cup, finished getting dressed, and then herded the dog and cat into the car. Once he'd dropped them off and gotten a tight hug from his mom—although he was almost certain she was happier to see Fenrir and Hel than him—Mat headed into Hidden Harbor. Was his mom right? He was already worried about what Niall might uncover when it came to Ana Hamarsson. Did he need to worry about how this newly discovered half brother of Niall's would react to learning about him?

AS IT HAPPENED, Mat didn't have time to worry about Niall once he got to the station. Birdy was already there and waiting for him.

"Good morning, sir," she said with an early-bird-who'd-caught-the-fattest-worm smile teasing her lips.

Mat peeled off his jacket and hung it on his chair.

"Morning. What have you found out?" he asked. He sat down and automatically grabbed his mouse to wake up his monitor.

"We have a tentative official ID from Dr. Soper based on the car's registration and Facebook pictures. Also, I called that restaurant a few minutes ago and asked about Hollis."

"Isn't it kind of early?"

"Possibly, but they serve lunch, and I thought maybe they

were the kind of place that had early deliveries or something. Anyway, the manager, Evi Jones, answered."

"And?"

"And Hollis took his boyfriends there quite often. It sounds like he had a pattern of sorts, like a serial dater. He'd bring a guy in and they would receive the star treatment for a few weeks or months. Then, like clockwork, he'd come in on his own for a little while before the cycle started again, only with a different boyfriend. He was a big tipper and a longtime customer, so they remembered him."

"Did you get any names? Or at least the most recent one?"

Birdy frowned. "That's where I hit a wall. It seems Hollis was in the no-boyfriend phase of his cycle. The last one stopped coming in a few weeks ago after they had a loud argument in the middle of the meal. And even when he was dating, it wasn't often that he introduced them to the staff. Which makes sense— after all, when you go to a place, do you introduce Niall?"

That tracked with the social media posts Mat had seen.

"But no chance they remember maybe hearing a name for the last guy he brought in?"

She shook her head. "Nope. But she's going to ask her staff just in case and get back to us."

"Dammit."

"Not for that one," she added smugly.

"Deputy Flynn, are you holding out on me?"

"About a year ago, one stuck around longer than the rest. Evi remembered the name because he sounded like a '60s film star, Xavier Stone. Not only did Stone last longer than usual, but she said Hollis seemed legitimately distraught when they split up. Well," Birdy amended, "*pissed off* were the words she used."

"Huh. Have you tracked down Stone yet?"

"No, sir. I was waiting to connect with you first. I just got off the phone with Evi."

"I'm gonna spend the rest of the morning harassing everyone I can at the state for the video we need. See if you can't figure out any of the other boyfriends' names. Seems to me that a year is a long time to wait if this was a crime of passion. I'll see if I can find Stone's number and give him a call after I talk to the state. I want you to chase down that possible gun permit. Have we heard back from them yet?"

"Yes, sir, and will do, sir."

MAT KEPT the receiver pressed against his ear as he listened to the voice on the other end tell him they were going to have to wait for the video. The state refused to budge. Proper channels, blah blah blah. It infuriated Mat when people threw protocol at him as an excuse for being assholes.

"Breathe in, sir. Your face is turning red." Birdy looked slightly alarmed.

Carefully, Mat set the handset back down in its cradle. As much as he wanted to throw it across the room, there was nothing in the budget for a new phone. He settled for picking up his pen and jabbing it against the top of his desk.

"If we could take a look at the damn video, we'd be that much closer to tracking down our killer. At this point, everyone we want to talk to lives three or more hours away."

And the perp had very likely left the island already. The ferry had already sailed and returned eight times since yesterday morning, sometimes stopping at the other islands, sometimes going directly to Anacortes. Still, regardless of the circumstances, he and Birdy would try their best to figure out who had murdered Arsen Hollis.

Birdy looked at him expectantly.

"How about you call Xavier Stone now?" she suggested. "I'm still hitting a blank wall on any other prior boyfriends' names."

"He's probably an asshole too," Mat griped.

She didn't reply; instead, Birdy opened the bottom drawer of her desk and took out a jar that Mat hadn't seen for a while.

"That's not anything Evi hinted at," Birdy replied, setting the swear jar on Mat's desk with a thump. "I thought I'd call the businesses located on either side of Hollis's brokerage, to see if they might have any information for us, before I went looking for more names of past dates. We still haven't been able to locate a relative or anyone else to let them know of his death."

Next, Birdy pulled out a notepad, carefully wrote a phone number down on it, tore the page off, and handed it to Mat. As he often did, Mat counted his lucky stars that Birdy Flynn wanted to stay on Piedras and not move to a bigger city with more opportunities. Thank god for Leo Zelinsky, who'd managed to romance Birdy into a serious relationship. And since Leo had moved to the island, Birdy was staying too.

Pulling out his wallet, he plucked a dollar bill out and dropped it into the jar. Then he picked up the phone again and pressed in the string of numbers.

Seconds later, the words "Xavier Stone" came over the line. Mat was mildly surprised; he'd expected to leave a voice message.

"Mr. Stone, this is Mat Dempsey, Piedras County Sheriff. Do you have time for me to ask you a few questions?"

"Piedras County? Where the hell is that? I don't think I could be in trouble there." He paused. "I suppose it's possible though. Sure, let me get inside. I was just walking my dog." Mat heard some scuffling in the background. "Lebowski, get your fluffy ass over here right this minute! Sorry, he's the laziest dog on the planet except when he's on a walk."

There were more puffing and bumping sounds and then Stone was back. "Okay, then. How can I help you?"

There was no subtle way to ask questions like "When did you last see your ex-boyfriend?" so Mat didn't bother trying to ease into it.

"Are you acquainted with an Arsen Hollis?"

"Oh, fuck me, what has the Ass Hole done now? Get it? AH? Ass Hole?" Stone snorted at his dad joke. "I haven't seen or talked to him since last fall when he dropped by for a very unwelcome visit. What a — look, I know it's not PC, but he's a douche in the absolute worst way. The best thing I ever did was break up with him."

There was no bitterness in his tone. Stone wasn't the one who'd been left behind. Mat mentally checked the man off their list.

"I hate to do this over the phone, but Arsen Hollis died yesterday. Here on Piedras Island. Well, actually on the ferry, but it's my case."

What followed was what Mat could only call a stunned silence.

Finally, Stone spoke. "What? Arsen's dead? What happened? Was he murdered?"

Mat met Birdy's curious gaze and shook his head. Unless this guy was a great actor, he was honestly shocked by the news of Hollis's death.

"That's what we'd like to know. At this time, we're treating it as a suspicious death."

"It wasn't me. Wait, I'm sure everybody says that. But I was glad to wash my hands of the man. He wasn't worth the time and effort it would take to get away with murder."

"Do you have time for me to ask a few more questions? It might help us find the killer if we know more about Mr. Hollis. Does he have a relative we can notify?"

"Um, sure. I don't know about any relatives, but I can talk with you."

Instead of lurking in the taproom for two hours, Niall ate his chili, paid up, and spent some time exploring the neighborhood around downtown Collier's Creek. Mat would like the town, so he did his best to see it from his husband's perspective—not his own, which was decidedly less rose-tinted.

As he wandered, Niall stopped in front of an old-timey storefront and found himself intrigued by the Collier's Creek Historical Society and Museum. After paying the five-dollar entry fee, he ended up spending an hour inside, engrossed by pictures of the Old West and the White settlers who'd claimed the area as theirs when they'd arrived.

It was just after four when Niall left the museum. His stomach was jittery, a feeling he wasn't used to. What the hell did he think he was doing? What if this relation—this unknown half brother—wanted nothing to do with Niall? Why was he going to all this effort?

When Niall had been twenty-four—a fucking lifetime ago—he'd already been on the Seattle police force for a year, determined to Protect and Serve, his life choices forever molded by a mother who'd abandoned him and an unnamed police officer who'd come to his rescue. Had Ana also abandoned *this* son, or by some miracle had she cleaned up only to come to a terrible end?

There was only one way to find out, and that was why he was in Collier's Creek.

Snapping out of his thoughts, he looked up and saw he had made it back to the taproom.

"Now or never, I suppose."

Pulling open the door, he stepped inside Jake's Tap for the second time that day. It was busier now and he was able to sidle across to the bar area and toward a remaining spot without being greeted.

Tad from earlier was still working the taps, nodding at him when Niall took the last seat at the bar, and a second person also chatted with patrons and poured them beers. Niall didn't have to ask what that person's name was. He also knew the exact moment Dakota Green spotted him.

It felt like Niall'd taken a time machine back to when he'd been both young and angry. Admittedly, he often still simmered at a low boil for the most part, generally pissed off at the fucking world, but nothing like when he'd been younger.

Dakota Green was at least as tall as Niall. His shoulders were just as broad. His darker hair was short with the hint of a wave. His skin tone was lighter than Niall's, but other than that, it was remarkably like looking at himself in a mirror that looked backward in time. Niall noticed Tad looking from him to Green and back again; did he see the similarities between them as well?

Dakota set the pint glass he'd just filled down hard enough that liquid sloshed over the edge and onto the bar. Oh, yeah, the kid wasn't pleased to see him. Niall was mostly unperturbed. He had a lifetime of dealing with people who weren't happy to see him.

Of course, the person had never been a recently discovered half brother. He and Shay hadn't gotten along for years, but that was due to Shay and Niall having different opinions about law more than anything else. Shay had once told him that while police enforced laws, lawyers applied them—and there was a lot of wiggle room in the word *applied*.

Crossing his arms and leaning back slightly in his chair, doing his best to not come off as threatening, Niall gave Dakota plenty of time to approach him. When it appeared he planned to ignore Niall, Niall switched to plan B.

"Dakota Green?" Niall asked when Dakota served a patron just a few stools down the bar.

The kid looked as if he might deny his identity, but Tad shot him a quizzical frown.

"Yes."

Short. To the point. *Yes.* And he didn't want anything to do with Niall.

Too fucking bad.

"My name's Niall Hamarsson. Is there a place we can talk privately?"

Tad opened his mouth but Dakota shook his head. "No."

He wasn't going to argue. If the guy wanted to talk here, that was fine with Niall.

"Is Ana Green your mother?"

Dakota eyed him before slowly nodding. Niall could tell that he already knew, likely he'd instinctively known for years, that Ana was gone. Just like Niall had.

There was the first thing they had in common. The knowledge wasn't something Niall wished on anyone.

"I'm sorry to be the one to tell you this, but Ana's remains were recently identified." He paused in case Dakota wanted to change his mind about talking in public. Tad moved to stand at his side, giving him silent support. Niall appreciated the move and decided he liked him for it. "She was discovered in Barstow, California, several years ago, but no ID was found with her. I tracked you down as a favor to the police department there."

"Kota." Tad nudged him with his elbow. "They must have matched your DNA." He turned to Niall. "Kota sent in one of those genetic tests a couple of years ago."

"You must have checked the button allowing law enforcement to have access to it," Niall stated. The Wild West-tinged era of genetic genealogy was over; now donors had to explicitly authorize their DNA to be used in searches for criminals who'd left evidence behind. Or maybe he'd used one of the few companies that allowed results to be shared with LEOs because he'd already suspected Ana met with foul play.

Dakota's response was another shrug. The kid wasn't going to make this easy. Niall sent a quick mental apology to his—*their* —grandparents for being an asshole when he was young.

"I'm a forensic investigator," Niall explained, deciding to take the roundabout way to the rest of the news he had to impart. "The company I work for recently asked that I give a sample in case something happened at a scene and my DNA needed to be ruled out. It's fairly common practice these days."

"You guys are related, that's why you're here," Tad whispered, his eyes wide. "Are you Kota's dad?"

Niall stared up at the ceiling for a moment and then back at the two young men on the other side of the bar. He took a deep breath. "Dakota, the DNA test identified me as your half brother."

"HOW DID IT GO?" Mat asked when Niall called that evening.

Niall thought back to what he had been calling "first contact" with Dakota Green. "Imagine me at twenty-four. Only angrier and with fewer resources." At least he'd had his grand-parents.

Their grandparents.

There was silence on the other end of the line. "That bad, huh? Angrier and grumpier, didn't think that was possible. What are you going to do about it?"

Trust Mat, again, to get right to the heart of the matter.

The meeting hadn't gone well, but Niall was determined to be patient with Dakota Green. At least as patient as he could manage. He hadn't felt that way when he'd walked into the pub. But seeing his half brother scowling and fierce, reminding him of himself but possibly more damaged, had Niall changing tactics.

"I'm going to employ The Mat Dempsey Method."

Mat made a choking sound. "Ew, gross. You're related—and too old for a twenty-four-year-old. And married—to the one and only Mat Dempsey."

Smiling into the phone, Niall also rolled his eyes. "Fucker," he said without heat. "I left my card. On the back of it, I wrote down the names of a few people on the island he might like to meet. I also told him we'd be having a memorial for Ana in the next few weeks. Whether he'll show up or not, I don't know, but when we have a firm date, I'll leave a message at his work. I've reached out to Sage already. She and Marigold are going to come up with something appropriate."

What was an appropriate memorial for a person who hadn't lived life particularly well? Niall didn't know, but he trusted Sage and Marigold to do the right thing.

"He probably threw the card away already."

Niall nodded, his attention on Mat while he paced the room he'd rented at the Collier's Creek Bed and Breakfast. "Proba-bly," he agreed, "but I also gave one to his coworker and told him to give it to Dakota in a few days."

"Nicely done. Do you think he'll come to Piedras?"

Niall thought back to Dakota's reaction to his arrival. He'd had no trouble recognizing the volatile mix of anger and fierce hunger —he'd felt both all the way to his bones more times that he could count. Then there was how Dakota had shut Niall down, refusing to listen to what Niall had to say, but he'd also seemed to linger close enough to eavesdrop on the conversation between Niall and Tad.

"Maybe. Pretty sure he's been on his own for a while. If nothing else, curiosity will get the better of him." Curiosity must also be a trait he and Dakota shared. Niall had thought about offering to pay for the trip but suspected Dakota would refuse.

Mat didn't respond right away. Then he said, "When Mom finds out he's coming, she'll be making up the spare room."

"Just what Alyson needs, another lost soul."

"Hey," Mat protested. "I'm not a lost soul."

"You're the exception," Niall teased. "Nice, normal Mat Dempsey, whose moral compass is straight and true."

"Not straight," Mat muttered. "When are you coming home?"

Home. For so many years that had been a foreign word to Niall. Home was something he hadn't understood and certainly didn't think he deserved. Now Niall had a home—and the name of his home was Mat Dempsey. Although Piedras Island wasn't bad either.

"I have a flight to Seattle tomorrow. With any luck at all, I'll be back on the island by evening."

"Good, because Fenrir has decided he gets to sleep on your side of the bed when you're gone. Which means Hel also sleeps on the bed and I get about an inch of space."

"You could just kick them off."

Mat was a pushover. Neither the cat nor the dog tried to sleep on the bed when Niall was home.

"Fenrir always gives me a *look*. Like I'm the worst human who's ever lived when I say no."

Niall chuckled. "A *look*, huh?"

"Yes, a look."

"Anything interesting happening up there?"

Mat was silent for a second which meant that, yes, something was going on. Maybe he should have listened to the voicemail Mat had left.

"As a matter of fact, we had a murder on the ferry yesterday morning."

"What?" Niall lurched forward in the uncomfortable desk chair provided by the bed-and-breakfast. "How come you didn't tell me right away?"

"For one, you have a lot on your mind. For two, I'm more worried about what you're are doing and how you're feeling than about a dead guy who, it seems, very few people liked. I know that sounds a tad callous but that's how I'm feeling."

"Tell me what's going on," Niall demanded, rising to his feet and crossing to the window to look out over the quiet street lined with maple and alder trees. The trees were still bare—spring was near but hadn't arrived quite yet.

"Bossy much?"

"Yes."

He could almost hear Mat rolling his eyes as he answered.

"Arsen Hollis, forty-four. Home address in Olympia, an upscale condo near the harbor. He was a real estate broker and owned his own company. Also has property in Ruston. He was discovered by deckhands when his car failed to disembark. Close-range shot to the head. Car locked. Powder residue on his hands would mean suicide if we'd found the weapon. Let's see, what else? He was a flashy money spender. Nice car, nice clothes. Liked to wine and dine and has the social media posts to prove it."

"And?" Niall prompted.

"I talked to one of his ex-boyfriends earlier today, a Xavier Stone. He didn't have anything nice to say about Hollis. They haven't been together for almost a year though, and Stone is with someone else now. And he was the one who did the breaking up. But apparently, it was usually Hollis who got tired and dumped people."

"He sounds like a real gem."

"Yeah."

Niall related to the frustration he heard in that single word.

"The state's dragging its feet on surveillance video?" Niall knew it was.

"Yep. Probably could have this squared away already if we could just see who got on and off the ferry during that sailing. And no, you can't ask Ryder to look into it because whatever he found wouldn't be admissible. I'll just be patient."

Niall felt himself smile.

"Alright, I won't ask Ryder. But you know he'd do it in a second."

"I do know. Changing subjects, we're going to have to go to dinner at Mom's once you get back."

"That's not a problem." Just thinking about Alyson's home-cooked meals had his stomach growling.

"She's going to ask you a lot of questions."

"I know that as well. I'll do my best to answer them. But I'm holding out for paella."

"Who are you and what did you do with my husband?"

A snicker escaped him. "Don't worry, I'm right here."

He was back to thinking about how Ana had died, how her remains had been discovered, and wondered if the retired detective, Abe Black, would return his call. Ryder had tracked the man down, he had an address in Florida these days, but he was still searching for the Department of Transportation guy who'd found her remains.

"What do you think the chances are that you'll learn anything about Ana's death?"

Mat was reading his mind again. Niall stared into the dark outside the window of his room. One of the streetlights flickered and he saw an older woman walking what appeared to be a raggedy dust mop with teeth. He could hear its shrill barks from inside the room.

"I've got a call into the original investigating officer. If he doesn't get in touch tonight, I'll call again in the morning. Doesn't look good, but with any luck I'll learn enough to justify some digging. Ryder's poking around, you know he can't stand a mystery. But honestly? I doubt we'll catch whoever did this. I'm going to do what I can though."

"You're a good man, Niall Hamarsson."

"Hmm," Niall grunted. "I don't know about that. But no one deserves to be strangled, tied up, and stuffed into a culvert. That's just a sadistic asshole making a point about disposable people. Even if she hadn't been my mother, I would want to find who did this."

"It's been a long time."

"Yeah. I guess it all depends on whether the detective has anything he wants to share with me that wasn't in the file."

"AM I SPEAKING TO DETECTIVE BLACK?"

There was a brief silence before the man on the other end of the call replied.

"Been retired for a while now, but that used to be me."

Black's voice was gravelly and rough, like he'd had a three-pack-a-day habit for years. Maybe he still did.

"Niall Hamarsson. I used to work homicide in Seattle. Now

I'm with West Coast Forensics. We're a private consulting company—"

"I've heard of West Coast," Black broke in. "What case are you calling me about?"

"One of your last. A woman's remains found in a culvert outside of Barstow."

Black was quiet for a while. Niall could hear him breathing, so he hadn't hung up.

"Right. I remember that one." Black probably remembered all his cases, especially the unsolved ones. Niall could relate. "Nobody came forward to ID her and there wasn't enough left for us to take fingerprints. We ran an artist rendering in the local paper, but that got absolutely nothing, and it wasn't picked up by the national news."

"Well, as it turns out, the victim was my mother. The case came up as part of an effort to ID cold cases."

More silence met Niall's announcement.

"I'm sorry, son," Black eventually said, his voice possibly more gravelly than before. "But she finally has a name, that's good."

True. A name meant that Black at least was closer to closure. It was more than the Doe file Niall had been working on.

"I always figured something bad had happened to her," Niall told the detective. "But I didn't know which was worse, that she was likely dead, or that she'd abandoned me and found a happier life. Unfortunately, it seems as if it was both. Found out there's another son as well, younger than me." The only reason Niall could explain the unusual personal info dump was that he felt an affinity for the old cop.

"Another son," Black repeated. "Damn."

"Yep. There's quite an age gap between us so Ana

Hamarsson—that was her name—did find something else, for a few years anyway."

"I hate to say this, kid, but I don't think she was happy. Did you read the autopsy report?"

Niall almost cracked a smile at the old detective calling him a kid.

"I did."

"Then you know there were signs of long-term drug abuse."

"Being an addict doesn't mean Ana deserved her fate."

"No. No, it doesn't. I didn't mean to imply that. I just meant that she might not have associated with people who meant her well."

Since that had generally been Ana's problem—associating with users and criminals—Niall had held no illusions that she'd spent a lot of time with wholesome individuals after she left.

"Is there anything you can tell me that's not in the report? Witnesses? A gut feeling?"

In Niall's opinion, gut feelings were among an investigator's strongest tools if used alongside solid data. He gave time for the retired detective to think, squashing down his natural impatience. Ana had been dead for almost a decade, and hurrying Black would get Niall nowhere.

"It had been raining for days, I remember. Maybe almost two weeks, unusual for Barstow. When the call came in, I was working the late shift so I was the lucky one." he paused, clearing his throat. "I got out there and met the construction worker."

"I thought he worked for the city?"

"Yeah, maybe he did. He'd been checking culverts and storm drains, clearing them out so they wouldn't overflow onto the roadways. It seemed like several had already done that."

"Happens at home too."

"It was still pissing down outside. I remember that clearly. The guy—what was his name?"

"Jack Wilson. That's what was in the file."

"Right. Jack Wilson. I remember thinking he might've well had been named John Smith his name was so common. Maybe his parents were tired of thinking up names or something by the time he came along."

Niall rumbled a sound of agreement, wanting Abe to hurry up but also wanting to not interrupt his memories.

"The instant I stepped out of the cruiser, I was soaked. The rain pissed me off because I'd worn new shoes that day and they were toast. I remember thinking, Jesus, Abe, get a damn grip, someone died out here. Just one of those moments, you know?"

Niall did know. He had several cases that haunted him and he recalled individual moments from each of them. The worst was Tania Nichols, made even worse because they knew who the perp was but any evidence had been scattered across acres of forest by birds and other small creatures.

"Didn't take me more than a glance to know it was bad. Called in the rest of the team."

Niall knew from the file that a coroner had responded along with an evidence crew. He'd track the evidence folks down if he had to, but the coroner had passed away a few years ago.

"Did this Jack Wilson guy have anything to say aside from what you noted?"

"Not that I recall. He wanted to get along to the next culvert since it was still raining. In all my years, I can't recall a wetter, more depressing scene. I finally let him go do his job so more roads wouldn't flood. He came in the next day and gave a pretty straightforward statement. He'd been assigned that area to check and clear stoppages and was the unlucky one to find the body. Apologies." There was a hint of a mental shrug. "You know how it is."

Niall did. He couldn't fault him.

"I have one of my guys looking for Wilson, but he seems to have dropped off the map. Do you remember if he was a city or state worker or a contractor? San Bernardino County uses a mix of them."

Niall'd had time to do a little research while waiting for his plane to Jackson and now it was coming in handy.

"He had one of those white trucks like they all do. Wore a high-vis vest."

"Did the truck have anything on the side? A city seal or something? Might give us a direction to look."

Black was quiet for a while. Niall tapped his fingers restlessly against the desk.

"I don't remember. It was just one of those white city pickups with all the gear in the back."

MAT

"So," Mat said around a bite of sandwich, "Stone didn't have much helpful to add. Apparently, Hollis showed up in Cooper Springs last fall with someone Stone didn't know and didn't ask to be introduced to. Stone thought Hollis was trying to make him jealous but it didn't work because Stone's had enough of Hollis to last a lifetime. And he—Stone—is happy in a new relationship. He did agree to come and officially identify the body. He'll be here tomorrow."

"Hmm." Birdy looked thoughtful. "He's our best lead, yet he says he hasn't had contact since last fall."

"I believe him."

Mat swallowed and took a gulp of water from one of the fancy PCSD water bottles that the county had bought for them —instead of something useful like more evidence collection kits. "It does give us more insight into Hollis as a person. Sounds like he was a jerk, but that doesn't give a person license to kill."

Without the ferry video, they'd hit a wall. No one had called back from the real estate agency Hollis owned, making Mat think he was right and Hollis was the only employee. It would be great if they could find his phone.

"Stone did say that Hollis was more attached to his cell phone than his mother," he added.

"Did Stone know anything about Hollis's relatives?" Birdy asked.

"Nope. He—Hollis—never talked about family. Stone had the impression they were dead or at the very least estranged."

Mat's desktop chimed. Pushing his sandwich and drink aside, he found the mouse and clicked the screen awake. He hoped it was a message from the state, but it was more likely some spam that had wormed its way into his inbox instead.

His attention landed on the subject line, and he sucked in a breath. "It's from the ferry system folks."

He clicked the email open. Birdy rolled her chair closer to read over his shoulder, just as invested as Mat was. Quickly, he scanned the contents of the email, his half-eaten roast beef sandwich turning to rock in his stomach.

"Are you fucking kidding me?" Mat jabbed his finger at the screen, making it briefly turn a weird blue color where his index finger poked it. "Are they fucking kidding?"

Birdy leaned over and peered at his screen. "No, sir, I don't think they are."

"The video camera on the lower car deck wasn't working yesterday?" Mat glared at the screen, unable to believe what he was reading.

"That does appear to be what they are saying, sir."

The Washington State Ferries system was in a freefall of decay—everyone knew that. The fleet was aging fast, the last new boat having been built in the 1980s, and they all had mechanical problems more often than not. Currently, the Piedras route, which historically had four boats, was down to two due to maintenance issues. It was worse in other places, Mat knew, but Piedras had the longest route and the most people dependent on the ferries to get them to and from the mainland.

"How hard is it to maintain a fucking video camera?"

Birdy had let the first couple of fucks slide but now she pushed the swear jar into his line of sight.

Mat sighed and fought a yawn as he sat back and pulled out his wallet, dropping a twenty inside the glass container. "Paying it forward."

"I don't think you're using that phrase how it's meant to be used," Birdy said with a smirk.

"I suppose not." He stood up. "I need a coffee. And then what do you think about paying our local realtor a visit? Maybe he can help us learn more about Hollis."

"Maybe," Birdy added as she rose to her feet. "You think maybe Hollis was supposed to meet him? What if he was looking at property or something?"

"Great idea."

CARLSON REALTY WAS JUST two blocks up the hill from the station and along the way was the Jewel Creamery, which made the best ice cream on the island and the best coffee. When Niall was away on a job, Mat often stopped in even though they had a perfectly good espresso machine at home.

He opened the aqua-blue door and stepped inside the small space. The shop was tiny but well laid out. There were three small tables to sit around inside and the same number lined the windows outside, but mostly the owner encouraged patrons to get back outside and enjoy the sights.

A slender man of medium height and with raven-black hair greeted him from behind the counter with a smile and a waggle of his eyebrows. "Hey, Sheriff."

Benny Brambilla couldn't help but flirt. It seemed to come

to him as easily as breathing. It never bothered anyone since they all knew that Benny was head over heels in love with Teagan Morrison.

"Hey, Benny, how're things? They don't usually let you out of the barn, do they?"

Benny and Teagan owned Jewel Dairy, from which Jewel Creamery got its name and the dairy milk used to make its famous ice cream.

"They do when Ciara and her sexy husband are in Hawaii," Benny replied.

"I'm sure Teagan loves that."

Mat and Teagan were close to the same age and had both grown up on Piedras, although Teagan was a little younger than he was. Like Mat, Teagan had moved away from Piedras and gone into law enforcement, but he had suffered a career-ending injury that brought him back. Or maybe it was his father passing away and leaving the farm to him, Mat didn't know for sure. Teagan and Niall had a lot in common. They both snarled first and asked questions later.

Benny shrugged, still smiling. "It's all good. It means he misses me all day. What can we get you?"

"A double espresso for me and whatever Deputy Flynn is having. It's my turn," he said to Birdy before she could protest.

Rolling her eyes at him, Birdy ordered an iced coffee. Once they had caffeine in hand, they waved goodbye to Benny and headed up the street.

Carlson Realty was one of the older businesses in Hidden Harbor—in fact, on all of Piedras Island. Like many real estate businesses, Carlson featured local properties on the front window for passersby to see and be enticed by. Even though it was only March, there seemed to be quite a few listings posted, ones from the other islands as well as Piedras.

"Shall we?"

Birdy nodded and Mat opened the door, gesturing for Birdy to go inside ahead of him.

The interior of the office space harkened back to the 1970s and was definitely on the dingy side. The walls were covered with faux wood paneling, and cheap picture frames displaying properties for sale hung on them. There was also a large desk with no one behind it, although a bell had rung, so presumably there was someone in the back office to greet them.

The most recent Carlson descendant, and current owner, hadn't done much to update the place. Although, if they were selling houses, why would they have to? Visitors to Piedras were ensnared by the natural beauty and community on the island. They didn't care about the interior of an agency, they only wanted to plop down a wad of cash and be on their way.

A rustling and muttered curse preceded Carlson entering the room.

"Howdy, Chief Dempsey, what brings you in today? I don't suppose Hamarsson's decided he wants to put that property of his up for sale?"

The waterfront property left to Niall by his grandparents was worth a lot. He was constantly refusing offers for it.

Mat snorted as he shook his head. "Nope."

"Ah, well." The realtor shook his head. "Man can always dream. What can I do for you?"

"I'm sure you've heard about the incident yesterday morning?"

"The murder on the nine o'clock sailing? Sounds like an Agatha Christie mystery, doesn't it?"

Mat leaned one hip against the countertop while Birdy looked at the listings on the walls.

"It does. Too bad we don't have a Miss Marple or Hercule Poirot to solve it. It turns out the victim was a real estate agent and we're trying to find out why he was visiting the island. We were wondering if perhaps he'd had an appointment to meet with you and look at properties."

Carlson pursed his lips and tapped on the counter as if the motion would jog his memory.

"I don't think I had anything scheduled. But I can check the appointment book. It's possible that Diane made an appointment and didn't tell me. I would've been here all day yesterday anyway. Getting ready for the season."

"I'd appreciate it if you would check your book," Mat said as he leaned casually against the counter.

"What name am I looking for?"

"Arsen Hollis. He had his own brokerage if that helps."

"One moment."

Carlson disappeared into the back, reappearing seconds later with a tattered, three-inch thick, spiral-bound appointment book. He caught the look Mat gave it.

"I know, I know. Believe me, Diane has told me enough times. But I like writing things down the old-fashioned way. Computers have a way of eating things."

Mat chuckled. He could relate. "I still take handwritten notes. Mind, I have to transcribe them later, but I think it helps me remember things."

"That gives me some faith in humanity." Carlson flipped the book open to the correct section, then placed his finger on the page and dragged it down as he looked at each entry. Mat did his best to read it upside down, surprised by the number of appointments Carlson had listed.

"I'm not seeing anything for yesterday."

"What about today? Or even the next couple of days?"

Carlson flipped the page forward. And then the next page.

"Nope, still nothing." He kept flipping forward, the pages showing fewer and fewer entries until there were none. "Nothing at all for an Arsen Hollis."

"Damn," Mat said straightening away from the counter. "I was hoping, but I knew it was a long shot."

"I wish I could be more help. When Diane comes back, I'll ask her about the name. Maybe she forgot to write it down. Probably pigs will fly before she forgets to note something, but you never know."

"If you wouldn't mind."

"Not at all, happy to be of help."

"Where to next, sir?" Birdy asked when they were back outside.

Mat looked up the street toward the island's high school and back down the hill where the ferry dock lurked, teasing him with its very existence. Who had murdered Arsen Hollis in plain sight?

"If it was premeditated, then whoever did it had to know the surveillance cameras were out of commission."

"In that case, the perp would almost have to be a ferry worker," Birdy pointed out.

Mat groaned. "Which means we need to question them again."

NIALL

The frenzied blare of cars honking followed by the crunch of metal meeting metal woke Niall from a restless sleep. For the shortest moment, he couldn't figure out where he was. Why was the room all wrong? The shadows he stared at every morning weren't there. He blinked against the assault of light—everything was far too bright.

Then it hit him. Collier's Creek, Wyoming. And something had happened on the street outside.

Swinging his sleep-pant-clad legs out from under the covers, he padded across the wool area rug to look out the window. Pulling the curtain aside, he found himself squinting against morning light glancing off freshly fallen snow.

What the fuck?

"Motherfucker. Isn't it March? Why the fuck is it snowing?"

The streets were covered with a thick layer of the tricky white stuff. His rental, parked by the curb, was buried. It must have started after he went to bed and kept going all night. Unless there was a miracle thaw, he wasn't leaving Collier's Creek in the next few hours, not even today.

"Dammit."

The cause of his rude awakening was obvious. The street in front of the bed-and-breakfast was blocked by a newish silver sedan and a forest service green pickup truck that wasn't much younger than Niall. He couldn't see how they'd managed to crash on a mostly flat and empty street, but stranger things happened at home.

It didn't appear anyone was hurt.

"Dammit," he grumbled.

Turning away from the window, he hurriedly pulled on his clothes and heavy boots. Once he had on his coat and gloves, he made his way quickly down the stairs, where he spotted the owner of the bed-and-breakfast bundled up and just opening the door.

"Hell of a way to wake up," Delores said, echoing Niall's thoughts.

Together they made their way down the walkway to the street. The driver of the truck was already out from behind the wheel and checking his vehicle for damage. Niall doubted there was any. The sedan, on the other hand, had not fared as well. The hood was crunched in on one side and would need body-work—if the insurance didn't just write it off as totaled.

Delores sighed. "Geraldine!" she called out. "What are you doing driving in these conditions? Didn't Sheriff Morgan warn you about getting into any more incidents? I know he did."

The diminutive older woman behind the wheel opened her mouth to answer, but a shrill yip cut through the air and the dog —or mop—Niall had seen yesterday jumped onto the driver's lap and set its paws on the door frame, clearly planning its escape. Spotting Niall and Delores, the dog began savagely barking their direction. The driver grabbed a hold of it to keep it from jumping out.

"That's Barky," Delores said. "He has an attitude problem."

"And he should be secured in a carrier, or at the very least, a dog seat belt," Niall added.

Geraldine's gaze flew to Niall. She started as if noticing him for the first time.

"Barky doesn't like the harness," she said. "And I was only heading to the feed store in case the snow sticks."

The low whine of a police siren reached their ears and Geraldine visibly deflated.

The sheriff's cruiser stopped behind the sedan and a tall, dark-haired man got out and approached Geraldine's car. He shot Delores and Niall a grimace before leaning into the driver's side window.

"Geraldine."

Barky, perhaps sensing his fate was in the balance, wiggled out of Geraldine's grasp and jumped out of his owner's hands and into the back seat.

"Um, hi, JD."

"Are you alright?" he asked, the concern in his voice laced with irritation.

She nodded, looking as guilty as a kid caught stealing candy.

"I'm fine," Geraldine insisted. "The sun came out all of a sudden and it was shining right in my eyes. I couldn't see. Then... boom," she finished glumly.

"That dog needs to be restrained while you're driving. We've talked about this before. And you shouldn't be on the road today, not while the conditions are sketchy."

The driver of the truck hurried over. Niall recognized Tad, one of the bartenders from Jake's the day before. He shot Niall a questioning look but didn't say anything.

"Um, hi, Sheriff Morgan."

Tad was probably the same age as Dakota, Niall figured, or close to it. Niall appreciated that he didn't seem angry about the accident; in fact, he suspected Tad was more concerned about Geraldine than anything else at the moment.

Morgan straightened and looked over at him. "Tad, that your truck?"

"Yeah."

Tad stopped next to the sedan, his gloved hands jammed into the pockets of his down jacket.

"You okay?" Morgan asked.

"Yeah, the truck is too. You alright, Geraldine?" Tad peered into the car.

She nodded. "Just my pride is dented—and the hood of my car."

"Geraldine says the sun got in her eyes."

"It got pretty bright," Tad agreed, "but I was coming the other way. Could've happened to anybody."

Morgan's gaze slid to the dog in the back of the car and back to the driver. Geraldine smiled up at him, batting her massive false eyelashes. Niall caught Delores's skeptical gaze and quashed the desire to roll his own eyes. This was why Mat was the sheriff on Piedras and Niall stayed behind the scenes with West Coast Forensics. He did not have the patience that people like Mat and JD Morgan had.

"Alright. I won't give you a citation this time, Geraldine, because I think having to have your car fixed is lesson enough." He patted the roof of her car. "You want me to call Walt?"

Niall assumed Walt drove a tow truck.

"Who wants coffee while we wait? Walt and his crew are going to be busy, so it might be awhile," Delores said. "The pot had just finished brewing when I heard the commotion out here."

To Niall's surprise, everyone wanted coffee, even Tad. Once they were inside—Delores reluctantly agreed that Barky could also come in and Morgan asked if he could fill his to-go cup because the machine at his office was broken—Tad sat down next to Niall at the oak table in the bed-and-breakfast's formal dining room.

"Is Dakota doing alright?" Niall asked so the kid wouldn't have to dance awkwardly around the topic.

Tad sipped his coffee and chewed on the inside of his lip before answering. Abruptly, Niall realized that Tad had been on his way to talk to him. Standing at the buffet, Morgan looked up while in the midst of filling up a to-go cup larger than any Niall had seen before and Delores hovered close by, ready to start another pot.

"What's up with Green?" Morgan asked sharply.

Tad glanced from Morgan to Niall and back again, clearly unsure how to answer or what to say if he did.

Niall stood from his seat and extended his hand toward Morgan. He should have stopped by and let them know he was in town and what he was doing there yesterday. Barstow had called ahead, yes, but it was still professional courtesy.

"Niall Hamarsson. I'm with West Coast Forensics, but I'm here in town on personal business. Detective Garcia from Barstow should have called to let you know I was coming."

Morgan narrowed his eyes. "Sounds familiar. You're doing a family notification?"

"Yes." He snapped his lips closed around the word. Dakota Green didn't need his personal business—which was also Niall's—being aired over coffee.

"I see. Thank you for taking the time to come and do it in person." Morgan snapped the lid back onto his giant insulated caffeine delivery system. "It's time I got back outside, but stop by the station before you leave if you have the time."

Morgan said goodbye to Julia and Geraldine, ignoring Barky, and was out the door, but Tad lingered. Niall motioned for the young man to follow him to the guest sitting room where they could talk more privately.

"You were coming to see me, right?" Niall asked, choosing to stand in the middle of the room instead of risking sitting on one of the delicate-looking sofas situated near the fancy pellet stove. "How'd you know where I was staying?"

Tad raised an eyebrow. "In March? In this town? All I had to do was ask."

"Makes sense." He'd failed small talk class so just dove to the heart of the matter. "What's going on with Dakota?"

"I don't know. He won't talk to me. He's mad, I'd guess. Are you really his half brother? I mean, you guys look alike, so yeah, I guess you could be, but—"

"What?"

"You're a lot older than Kota." Tad shrugged. "I'm worried about him, that's all. He's never had anybody, not really, and now you waltz in and tell him stuff about his mom and that you're related and... you're just going to leave again? What good is that?"

Fuck. Niall sighed. This was going to be a longer conversation than Niall had initially thought. He might even need to risk sitting down.

"You and Kota are friends? Good friends?"

Something in the kid's expression, the almost unnoticeable flush coloring his sharp cheekbones, had Niall thinking that Tad possibly thought of Dakota as more than a friend.

Also, note to self: neither of them are kids. They are twenty-something young men. He managed to suppress his groan at the thought.

"Yeah, we're good friends," Tad said slowly. "He, uh, lived on my family's ranch for a while. After... after his mom left. She lived there too, before. She cooked and cleaned the house, but then one day she was just gone."

Niall chose a settee and eased himself down. It creaked underneath him. The thing was made for tiny women who knitted and drank tea, not him.

"Do you think he'll come to the memorial?"

Tad shrugged. "It's not like he has a lot of money."

"Ana abandoned me too," Niall stated baldly, watching Tad's eyes widen slightly at his words. "She was sixteen when I was born and she'd run away from home. No one knew she was going to have a baby. Eventually, when I was around six or seven, she abandoned me in downtown Seattle."

"Oh," Tad said quietly.

"I ended up in foster care for a short time. Luckily, my grandparents learned of my existence and took me into their home. Our grandparents, I suppose." There was no doubt in Niall's mind. If Od and Jo had known about Dakota, they would have taken him in as well. "There are still people on the island who knew Ana, and the memorial is mostly for them. To be honest, I don't have good memories of her. If Dakota does, I'm sure those people would like to hear them. And maybe he'd like to meet them too."

Until recently, Niall would never have been able to stay calm and rational about the situation he found himself in. He probably wouldn't have traveled to Collier's Creek either. He'd been happy to keep his head down and ignore everything. Mat Dempsey was to blame for this change of heart.

"Like I said yesterday, Dakota is more than welcome, but I'm not going to call him every day and beg that he come. He comes or he doesn't. It doesn't matter to me." Maybe he wasn't as calm and rational as he'd thought. "Maybe it will give him some closure," he added.

Mat was always going on about closure and how important it was to resolve things. Personally, Niall enjoyed stewing and plotting the imaginary death of his enemies, but Mat was probably right.

"Try and convince him to come," Niall said. "I'm not saying it will be easy or even fun, but he might benefit from meeting the family there. Two weeks from Sunday. If the date changes, I'll call Jake's and let you know."

Delores stuck her head around the door. "Are you boys doing okay in here? Walt's outside hooking up Geraldine's car, so I'm going to give her and that damn dog a lift to the feed store and then back home. Shouldn't take me more than a half hour."

"Bye, Delores," Tad said.

"You say hi to your mom for me, alright, Tad? Tell her we need to get our knitting nights going again."

"Yes, ma'am."

Delores disappeared and a few minutes later, Niall heard the slam of the front door and footsteps on the crunchy snow outside.

"What's the forecast today?" he asked Tad.

"Who knows? March in Wyoming means anything goes. You know what's weird?"

Niall shook his head—everything was weird at the moment.

"Dakota just graduated from Central Wyoming College with a degree in criminal justice. He's always wanted to be a cop."

MAT

Mat resisted the desire to pinch the bridge of his nose and squeeze his eyes shut. He was frustrated.

Birdy had spent the better part of the late morning and early afternoon re-interviewing the various ferry workers, at least the ones who were on their shifts. She'd sailed to Anacortes and back twice. Unfortunately, a couple of the crew were enjoying their days off and another had called out sick. None of the remaining folks had anything new to share about Arsen Hollis or finding his body.

"Nothing, nothing, and nothing. That was a waste of your time," he complained. He'd spent that time doing administrative crap, responding to a few minor incidents and one fender bender in the Chester's Grocery parking lot. He hadn't wanted to be trapped on the ferry if he was needed; instead, he'd spun his mental wheels.

"It wasn't, sir. You know that."

He did know, but the point was that it felt like it had been a waste of limited resources. And he was off-kilter having Niall gone. Not just gone, gone and dealing with heavy family matters. They hadn't talked last night either, just texted, which was unsatisfying. It had merely been an exchange of *how was your day?* Fine. *Did you learn anything?* Not really. That was pretty much the conversation on both sides.

Mat did not like this.

"When is Mr. Stone supposed to arrive?" Birdy asked.

Mat looked at his watch. "He's on the next ferry, less than half an hour."

"Maybe he'll have information that will be helpful? It will be nice to have an official ID." Birdy liked to see the bright side of things, even when it was about murder. This aspect of her personality was just one of the things that Mat appreciated about his second-in-command.

For the past two days, they'd been investigating with the strong assumption that the victim was Hollis. It would be nice to at least have the assumption confirmed. Mat allowed himself to feel slightly hopeful that they might learn even more after interviewing Xavier Stone in person.

"It will, and an official ID will get the ball rolling on checking his bank records and finding out who Hollis's cell service provider was so we can request those records too. Any luck with business associates? Maybe a receptionist? Anything?"

"Not yet, sir, but I put those calls into the businesses on either side of his office address yesterday. I'm hoping someone will return my call by the end of the day."

"If you don't hear from someone by then, let's ask someone down there to ask around."

Olympia wasn't the literal end of the world, but going themselves would mean an entire day off the island. Mat hated the Everett-to-Olympia traffic corridor with a passion and being short-staffed right now made any day trips nearly impossible anyway. If he had to, he'd send Soren, but he didn't want to waste money sending Jorgensen down to ask questions that could be answered over the phone.

"I'm going to make a fresh pot of coffee. Want some?"

Birdy shook her head. "No thanks, I'm good."

"Quitter," he grumbled as he rose to his feet and headed toward their tiny break room. It was really just an afterthought, barely big enough for two people to stand in and watch the coffee brew. Which is what Mat was doing when Stone arrived.

XAVIER STONE WAS MAYBE a little older than Mat. His hair was streaked with silver and was either tousled from the wind or expertly styled, and one of his contrasting dark eyebrows had a scar bisecting it. He was a handsome, distinctive-looking man. Not as sexy as Niall but good-looking enough.

"This is Vincent Barone." Stone glanced at the muscly, well-built dark-haired man waiting just behind him. "My boyfriend. I hope you don't mind. We decided to make a weekend trip out of this unfortunate event."

Barone stepped forward and offered his hand for Mat to shake. "Do I say nice to meet you in a situation like this? And please, call me Vincent."

"You came up from Cooper Springs, right?" Mat asked.

"Yep. Three-hour drive and two ferry rides already today," Vincent confirmed. "We're both ready to stop moving for a bit."

Xavier nodded his agreement. "I've never been to Piedras before, but completely worth the trip. And I'm using it as an excuse to do some research. That probably sounds callous of me."

"It's not," Vincent said, giving his boyfriend a fond glance. "Neither of us are mourning him, and we shouldn't pretend we are."

Vincent rested one hand against the small of Xavier's back,

and Xavier leaned into the touch ever so slightly. If it was possible, Mat missed Niall even more.

"This shouldn't take us long," Mat said. "An hour or so, I'd guess. Again, thank you so much for making the trip up here."

"I can't believe Arsen is dead," Xavier said, looking down at his obviously expensive footwear. "He was an asshole, but dead?" Looking back up at Mat, he shrugged. "I'm having a hard time wrapping my head around it."

That's because Xavier was a normal human being who (most likely) didn't resort to violence to solve his issues. Normal people used their words instead.

"Is there somewhere I can hang out while Xavier talks to you?" Barone wanted to know.

"If you're hungry, there's The Hook, a little café up the street. They have great grilled cheese," Birdy said. "If you just want good coffee, try the Jewel. The Jewel doesn't have much seating though."

Mat's stomach wanted a grilled cheese sandwich too, but that was going to have to happen after they'd been up to the hospital.

"Meet me at the café?" Vincent asked Xavier. "I could go for a sandwich or something."

"I'll let you know when I'm finished," Stone replied. "If it takes a long time, you could check in at the Brooch and then come back and get me. It doesn't look like a long drive on the map."

"You'll like the Brooch," Mat interjected. "And it's just a twenty-minute drive from here. But honestly, this shouldn't take long and then you can enjoy the rest of your stay on the island."

"THAT IS DEFINITELY ARSEN," Xavier said as he stared down at the body on the stretcher.

Mat glanced over at him. He looked a bit pale, but viewing a dead body would do that to a person. The doc had done a good job hiding the damage with creatively brushed hair.

Doc Soper nodded and wrote something down on the tablet he had in his hand.

"Thanks for doing the hard thing," Mat said to Xavier.

It had literally taken less than half an hour to confirm Hollis's identity. And that was only because Soper was with a patient in the ER when they arrived.

"What will happen to his body?" Xavier asked.

"Now that we know for sure who he is, we can start trying to find relatives," Mat answered. "With a little legwork and luck, someone will claim his remains and give him a proper burial or whatever he wanted."

"If you don't find anyone, let me know. He was an asshole, but I like to think he'd do something for me if our places were switched. I mean, he probably wouldn't, but I can pretend."

Xavier and Mat started to leave the room while Soper rolled the gurney back into the cold room where they kept the deceased. The door shut with finality. Now it was Mat's job to make sure a murderer didn't go free.

"If you could answer a few more questions," Mat said when they arrived back at the station, "that could be helpful to us. You'd be surprised how much you might know about Hollis that you didn't realize."

Mat glanced at his empty coffee cup and wished it would magically fill itself. Coffee would be his reward once the interview was over. And that grilled cheese sandwich. He sat down and gestured for Xavier to do the same.

"Mostly, I probably put him out of my head," Xavier said as he took the chair next to Mat's desk. "That man had one focus, the Arsen Hollis All The Time channel. At first, it seemed flattering, like he was sharing his life with me, but by the end, I basically tuned him out."

Opening the bottom drawer of his desk, Mat pulled out a fresh yellow legal pad for notes. Setting it down, he selected one of the pens his niece had given him for Christmas, scribbled on the top of the page, and was pleased when the pen left a black mark behind.

"How did you meet Hollis?"

Xavier glanced up at the ceiling. "We met at a business thing, a networking event for real estate agents."

"And you hit it off?"

"I guess. He asked me out. I was flattered because he was successful and had his own brokerage. I secretly wanted to be him." His eyes widened. "Not that I want to be him now, I mean. I'd be dead."

"What was your relationship like?"

"A lot of hot air, lots of posing, posturing. He liked the fact that he made more money than me. He liked making sure I knew he made more money. At first, I found his attitude a challenge. Like I could do that too, you know? I could make that kind of money. But the shine wore off pretty fast. Don't get me wrong, I like making money and he did teach me things about the industry but"—Xavier looked Mat directly in the eye—"the few times I closed a bigger deal or won a more impressive client, he was a total shit about it. Life is tough enough without someone who is supposed to be on your side undermining you."

"Did he do that much? Undermine you, I mean."

Xavier nodded. "Yeah, he went around my back a couple of times. Stole a client. It pissed me off at the time, but I obviously didn't kill him over it."

"How long ago was this?"

Xavier pursed his lips thoughtfully before answering. "Almost two years," he finally said, a sound of surprise lacing his tone. "I broke up with him too, and that royally pissed him off. I think he thought that I would just stick around and take his crap as long as he was dishing it out. Instead, I moved home to Cooper Springs and started over."

"Did he ever talk about family? Parents? Siblings? What about old boyfriends?"

Again Xavier took a minute before shaking his head.

"Nothing that comes to mind. I'm reasonably certain he didn't grow up in Washington State. I think he was an only child too. I have a twin brother and when I talked about Max— well, he was mostly jealous because Max is a genius tech millionaire, but he never said, 'Oh my sister this' or 'my brother that' like most people do."

"Parents?"

Xavier frowned. "I'm sorry. I just don't know?"

Mat asked a few more basic questions, but it seemed to him that Xavier Stone didn't know much about the man he'd once dated. He wasn't sure what that said about Xavier or Arsen.

"Our 'relationship' was based on making money and looking good while we did it. I'm not proud that I bought into the game. Not the finest time of my life," Xavier admitted. "I chose not to ask questions because I didn't care about him either, not really. I like to think I've changed since then. I'm pretty sure I have anyway," he added, then his eyes lit up. "Vincent seems to want to keep me around."

Sitting back in his chair, Mat idly tapped the legal pad, trying to come up with another question.

The pause gave Xavier time to think of something else. "That last time I saw Arsen, in September or so? I think he was trying to make me jealous or wishing I hadn't broken up and left Olympia."

"What happened?"

"He'd been calling on and off with the pretense of checking

in on me. As if I was devastated or something. I was ignoring his calls because he was just lording over me—how is your little business going? Shit like that, with the emphasis on little, like starting my own business was just a passing fancy. Anyway, he showed up with someone I assumed was a new boyfriend. Also probably to try and make me jealous."

"Did you get a name?"

"No, it was a short, unpleasant conversation. Vincent came to my rescue," Xavier said with a small smile.

"Have you and Vincent been together long?"

"We went to high school together, but between me being a self-absorbed ass and Vincent being smarter than that, it took us a while. We've been official for a few months now."

"Congratulations."

Mat saw Xavier's gaze darted to the picture of Mat and Niall on their wedding day. The picture had been taken after the short ceremony, thank god. For once in his life, Niall was smiling. Whenever Mat looked at the photograph, he thought Niall appeared slightly astounded that they'd gone through with it.

"That's Niall, my husband."

"Oh!" Xavier's grin was blinding. "That's amazing, what a wonderful shot! Congratulations." He leaned in, looking closer at the two of them. "He looks like the broody type. I bet he is, isn't he?"

"Well, not to talk about Niall when he isn't here to defend himself... but he does tend to brood a bit. He's..." What had Ryder said that had the entire West Coast Forensics team laughing so hard they couldn't breathe? Oh right. "One of his teammates compared Niall to Kimchi. 'He needs time to marinate and is definitely an acquired taste' was the exact phrase."

"Kimchi?" Xavier grinned. "That's hilarious."

"Yeah, and worse—or better, depending on who you are—

Ryder made a batch of kimchi at home and brought it into their office and made everybody try it so they knew exactly what he meant."

"So, your guy is slightly sour, with a little tang and some spice?"

Mat chuckled as he tossed his pen down on the desk.

"Yep, that's Niall."

NIALL

Niall breathed out a sigh of relief as he stared through one of the thick plate glass windows watching the ferry dock drawing closer with every passing second. Travel was fine, he did it for WCF often enough, but the weight that settled on his shoulders when he was away always lifted at the sight of the island he made his home on.

Luckily, he'd only had to stay one extra day in Collier's Creek. Tad had driven him to the airport in Jackson in exchange for Niall giving him some cash to give to Dakota in case he decided to travel to Piedras. Tad thought he would. Niall had no idea.

"He's a good guy," Tad insisted as he drove. "Just quiet. Doesn't like surprises much."

"I was a big surprise, I'd guess."

"That's an understatement. I don't know if he's more freaked out that he has a relative or that you're a cop."

"If it helps," Niall had told him, "I'm not a cop anymore."

The ferry bumped against the dock, dragging Niall from his thoughts. Overhead the mechanical voice reminded passengers that they needed to descend to the deck and offload before the vehicles. Clattering down the echoing metal staircase, Niall joined the other foot passengers to disembark.

As he strode up the loading ramp with his luggage bumping after him, Niall spotted Mat waiting in the passenger lot. His heart thumped hard at the sight of him.

"Hey," Niall said when he got to him, an unasked-for smile curving his lips. Mat was leaning against their battered Subaru, the car they shared when Mat didn't want to drive his assigned police vehicle. Sometimes it was nice to try and remind people he had a life outside of being the sheriff. It didn't usually work.

"Hey back." Mat straightened, taking Niall's roller bag from him and tossing it into the back of the car while Niall climbed into the front.

Even if Mat hadn't been the sheriff, Niall would still have waited to give his husband a proper greeting. The last thing Niall wanted was the gossips of Piedras acquiring more grist for the mill. *What was grist anyway?* He made a mental note to look the word up.

"How was the flight back?" Mat asked as he maneuvered the car out of the lot and into the meager line of cars heading onto Piedras.

"Fine. Just a long day." The Hook looked busy with late diners. "I keep thinking about the kid and wondering if he'll show up."

Turning right, Mat continued driving past the high school and toward home. "You think he won't?"

Niall shrugged. "No idea. I gave his friend Tad some money for travel. Maybe he can't leave his job. But obviously, I couldn't ask him. I did speak with Tad and encouraged him to try and get Dakota to come here."

"If he's anything like you, I think he'll come. If nothing else, the Hamarsson curiosity will make it impossible for him to resist. From the little you've told me, I have the feeling the two of you are a lot alike."

"Hamarsson curiosity, huh? Did I tell you he recently got a degree in criminal justice?"

Mat nodded. "Why doesn't that surprise me? An unsolved mystery or injustice is like catnip to you. I bet it's the same for the kid. I suppose I shouldn't call him a kid. He's an adult."

"I'm having the hardest time wrapping my head around the fact that Ana had another child," Niall admitted as he stared out the car window, watching the trees as they drove past. "What was she thinking?"

Mat didn't respond to his rhetorical question. There was no way for them to know what kind of life Ana had led after abandoning him. The only certainty was that she'd at some point taken the last name Green and had died violently in the end.

If Dakota decided to come to Piedras, Niall might get the chance to ask some of the questions he had. Growing up, he'd been angry about Ana's betrayal, angry that she'd dumped him like so much trash, angry that she'd left a trail of hurt humans in her wake. After learning that her spiral had begun after being seduced by Shay Delacombe's father—who was also Niall's father—the first cracks in his wall of unforgiveness had appeared.

Ana had been a vulnerable human and she'd been so young. Maybe she'd never had a chance. Even if his father had still been alive, Niall wouldn't have been able to forgive him. What David Delacombe had done was indefensible.

"We'll never know what she was thinking," said Mat, echoing Niall's thoughts.

"I told you I sent Ryder the files from Barstow, right? But yeah, I doubt even his special brand of research will find much. I talked to Abe Black, the original detective, and he didn't have anything new to say."

Mat turned down the drive that led to their home, the physical center of Niall's universe.

Damn, it felt good to be home.

The cabin his grandparents had built and lived in may have been gone, but he and Mat had built a new structure in its place. One big enough for the two of them, plus Fenrir and Hel. There was a spare bedroom too, although Niall didn't generally encourage visitors. Usually, guests stayed with Alyson, where they would be stuffed with delicious home-cooked meals and could enjoy her welcoming personality.

As he pushed open the car door, he was greeted by loud and enthusiastic barking emitting from the house, as if Fenrir knew Mat had brought Niall home.

"ARE YOU HUNGRY?" Mat asked once they were inside. "Mom sent some paella over."

Suddenly, Niall was starving, and his stomach rumbled accordingly.

"Yes," he confessed with a roll of his eyes.

Mat snickered. "How about I heat dinner up while you change or do whatever you want to do?"

With Fenrir at his heels, Niall headed into their bedroom and changed into a pair of comfortable jeans. He slipped a gray hoodie on over his Jewel Dairy t-shirt—the pink one with the three cows all wearing crowns. Ryder thought they were hilarious and had bought one for everyone in the WCF office.

Fenrir kept nudging his palm with his cold nose.

"What do you want?" Niall knew what the dog wanted. They always went down to the beach together after Niall got back from being away. It was their ritual. Sighing, he slipped on his boots too.

"Do I have time to take the wolf to the beach?" he asked.

Mat was standing at the stove, spatula in hand as he monitored their dinner. He glanced over his shoulder at Niall. "How about we eat down there?"

"Because it's March and I like my balls?"

"Your balls will be fine. If they get cold, I'll warm them up later." He waggled his eyebrows, making Niall smile again. "It's not frosty and you were just in Jackson, for crying out loud. You two—"Mat looked over at the small gray and white cat who was waiting by the door. "Pardon me, you *three* go ahead and I'll be there in a few minutes."

"As long as there's ball-warming in my future." Niall grabbed a couple of beach blankets off a shelf in the mudroom and stuck his toque on his head. "See you in a few."

He pulled the door open and Fenrir and Hel bolted outside as if it had been days, not an hour or so.

"Hey," he said to Mat.

His husband looked over at him. "Hey, what?" A little smile played across his lips as if he knew what Niall was about to say. He probably did.

"I missed you."

"I missed you too. I always miss you when you're off the island." Mat waved the spatula at him. "Get down to the beach before the Terrible Two do something we'll regret."

THEY'D WAITED for him as if going to the beach without him was impossible.

"You two are so weird. Tonight you're behaving?"

Together, Niall, Fenrir, and Hel made their way down to the rocky beach that was part of the property, their private slice of heaven. Mat had had the brilliant idea of putting solar torches along the path to light the way. The lights did their job and were dim enough that they didn't interfere with star-watching.

The tide was out but from the wave action, Niall thought it was getting ready to turn around and start back in again. Fenrir woofed and picked up his pace, trotting across the rocks to bark at the waves. Hel, deciding against getting wet, wandered over to the beach logs to watch her friend's antics.

"Me too," agreed Niall, sitting next to her. "It's too cold and no matter what Mat says, my balls are going to be chilly."

Mat was right, though, because it wasn't that cold. The ever-present wind was merely a gentle breeze, and the cloud cover helped to retain the warmth from the day. It felt like spring was on the way.

He didn't have to wait long for Mat. Only a few minutes passed before he heard the crunch of gravel under Mat's boots. Turning, Niall watched him step onto the beach, carrying the ridiculous wicker picnic basket Alyson had given them. The one they inexplicably used on a regular basis.

Setting the basket down by Niall's feet, Mat opened it and handed him a covered bowl and a fork before taking a bowl and fork out for himself. Niall held the bowl with both hands for a moment, savoring its warmth.

"This is perfect," Mat said as he sat down, bumping Niall's shoulder with his own.

"I don't disagree."

Fenrir spotted Mat's arrival and stopped cavorting with sea creatures, knowing there would likely be treats if he stuck close by. Niall peeked into the basket and sure enough, Mat had packed the container with Alyson's homemade dog treats.

"You spoil that dog," Niall said without heat.

"I'm not even going to respond to that."

They ate in relative silence punctuated only by the sound of the waves hitting the beach and their forks clinking against the sides of the bowls.

Finally, Mat set his empty bowl back in the basket.

"Beer?"

"Yes, please."

Beer in one hand, Niall set his bowl down as well.

"Well," Mat began, "you've had a few days now. What are you thinking for Ana's memorial?"

"Did Sage tell you we talked?"

"Maybe," Mat said with a smile.

"This island," he grumbled.

"This island that you love as much as I do."

"Yeah, yeah."

"Well?"

"Sage suggested a ship burial. A Viking send-off, of sorts."

He'd kind of done that before but maybe that didn't matter. This was for more people than just him.

"What do you think about that?" Mat asked.

He'd had time to think about it while making his way home.

"I think it's the right direction. A traditional memorial doesn't sound right to me. Sage thinks people who remember Ana could write a memory down on a piece of paper and then she'll put them all together. We'll build a small boat and load it with the memories, light it on fire and let them float out to sea."

"What if they write bad things? Just being devil's advocate."

"So what? Maybe whoever it is needs to get something off their chest. It's not as if I have pleasant memories."

"Do you have any good ones?"

Niall's mother wasn't a subject he and Mat discussed much, if at all.

Niall thought for a moment. He was almost forty-four years old, and his memories of Ana were blurred at this point.

"I have a vague memory of being with her outside somewhere. Maybe at a playground. She was smiling and it was sunny. I was happy."

"You should write down whatever you want, even if it's negative. Light it on fire and let the gods take care of the rest."

"I like how you avoid saying, 'that one time she locked you in a closet and there was a house fire.'"

"Best to let it go, don't you think?"

Niall nodded. "I do."

THE NEXT MORNING, Niall was at the table rereading an email from Sage on his laptop. The memorial for Ana Hamarsson was set for a Saturday afternoon ten days away. For whatever reason, having the date confirmed made the whole situation feel more real to Niall.

Ana Hamarsson was coming home. They were putting her to rest.

Sage had talked with her cousin, Cody Prescott. They would hold the memorial at the Brooch Resort, which Cody owned and ran. It was on the south end of the island and had enough space to hold everyone who might want to attend. Working with her cousin, Sage had been able to reserve part of the beach and obtain the permits they needed. Niall was infinitely grateful to the older woman for making sure the memorial was somewhere other than his and Mat's property.

He'd wanted to bring Ana home, just not to his actual home.

In addition, Cody had reserved several tables in the main restaurant for a casual meal afterward. Mat's family would be there, of course, as well as Shay, Ryder, and Claribel. Birdy Flynn and Leo and Birdy's brother, Devon, with his partner and WCF's other founder, Kimball Frye. The rest of the WCF staff that wasn't traveling for cases. And Stu Dennis as well. Along with Claribel Delacombe and Alyson, Stu was one of the few remaining residents on the island who remembered Ana. There were even extra seats allotted for last-minute additions. Sage felt it was important that anyone who wanted to say goodbye be allowed to do so.

There were now just two things bugging Niall.

Number one was Dakota Green. He hadn't heard anything from his half brother since he'd gotten home, and he couldn't decide if that was a good thing or not. Had he been too high-handed having Ana's remains sent to Piedras instead of giving Dakota a choice? After all, it seemed she had been much more of a mother to his younger brother than to Niall. Maybe she'd loved Wyoming. Niall had no idea.

"Quit overthinking," Mat said from the other side of the table. "I can feel it from here."

Niall didn't bother with a response. Overthinking was his superpower.

The second thing bugging him—not keeping-awake-at-night levels of bugging, more like a tiny sliver he couldn't get out of his finger—was the death of Arsen Hollis. Mat had shown him all the notes he'd taken and, much like Ana's case, nothing seemed to lead anywhere. Just one dead end after another.

The third thing niggling at him—as it had been for over a year—was the Doe case he'd taken on. Had he given it enough time? Had he really looked at every piece of evidence? He made a vow to go over everything, every bit of information, again.

"You can't make Dakota Green come here and you can't solve Hollis's murder by glaring at my notes. I'm sure there's something else going on in there too, but even my powers aren't boundless."

Huffing out a sigh, Niall slumped back in his chair, shooting an exasperated glance at his husband.

"Isn't it driving you crazy? Whoever murdered Hollis seems to have vanished into thin air."

There was no reason for Mat to know how invested Niall was in the Doe file.

Mat's dark eyebrows drew together. "Yes, it is driving me crazy. On the other hand…"

Niall sat forward, shutting his laptop. "What?"

"We got Hollis's bank records back today," Mat said smugly.

"You did? And?"

"And he was up to his eyeballs in debt. He'd been spreading money around to make minimum payments on what he owed and it looks like his condo payments were in arrears."

"The real estate market hasn't been kind recently," Niall said. "But being overextended isn't a motive for murder."

Even on Piedras, fewer people were buying these days and properties had been sitting on the market for much longer periods of time. Niall knew of several people who'd tried to sell and finally decided to wait until the market improved.

"But Hollis didn't have enough coming in and he was sinking fast. Maybe he owed the wrong person money? Maybe he was distraught?"

"Maybe he did kill himself," Niall agreed. "If he owed money to somebody shady, they sure aren't getting it now. You and I both know they'd rather have the money than a dead body."

"If it's an elaborate set up, a fake suicide, maybe Hollis was a write-off?" Mat suggested, but he didn't look terribly convinced. "Maybe they knew they weren't getting any money, so they took care of the problem."

"Mm, I don't buy it. If that were the case, they wouldn't take him out on a ferry boat, for fuck's sake. This feels like a crime of passion to me, or distress."

"I have to agree, but it still doesn't get us closer to the perp. And where did the weapon go?" The last was said with a growl. Mat was frustrated and had hoped the bank records would lead somewhere.

"A crime of passion with a lucky break," Mat grumbled. "Of

all the ferries in the system, he had to catch the one with nonfunctioning video cameras. And we still haven't talked to the last crew member again. I've got Birdy tracking down another means of contact."

Niall was fully aware that Mat was only allowing him to "interfere" with the Hollis case to keep his mind off the upcoming memorial and the problem that was Dakota Green. Little did he know that Niall could interfere with police work and worry about Dakota at the same time. He was a multitasker.

DAKOTA

Dakota Green scowled and huddled further into his heavy barn coat. The boat's engines rumbled underneath his feet and nerves were giving him goose bumps like he was cold and only anger kept him warm.

He really wasn't cold, not at all. The weather was practically balmy. He just had no idea what the fuck he was doing traveling to the northwestern tip of Washington State. This trip was not going to bring his mother back. If she'd been alive, he didn't know if he'd want her back in his life.

Leaving him behind had been unforgivable. Unspeakable.

The boat rocked slightly, and Dakota didn't like the sensation. Twenty-four years old and he'd never ridden on a ferry boat in his life, much less seen an ocean. At least, not that he knew of. Who knew, maybe he'd been to a beach as a baby. His mother had never talked much about their life after moving to Wyoming. His birth certificate said California but Dakota's own memories were vague. He frowned at the turbulent gray and green water on the other side of the plate glass window.

Really, what the fuck was he doing?

The guy who'd shown up in Collier's Creek—his *half*

fucking brother—hadn't asked him to drive a thousand miles and arrive unannounced. In fact, all he'd done was write some names on the back of a business card and inform Dakota that there'd be a memorial for his—*their*—mother as soon as possible.

Tad claimed it meant he should go. Ana was Dakota's mother too and he should at least say goodbye. Wasn't he curious where she'd come from? He—Niall Hamarsson—had even given Tad three hundred dollars in cash to give to him. Dakota had thought about refusing it, but Tad pointed out that it would make the trip and missing work easier. Tad had even offered to come along but Dakota didn't rely on people, not even his best friend, so he'd refused the offer.

And another thing. At the best of times, Ana Green had never been in the running for mom of the year, although he'd usually had a roof over his head, food, and clean clothes. But after doing the bare minimum for fourteen years, she'd just up and left Dakota at the ranch she'd worked at for a summer and never returned. Did she deserve a memorial? Dakota's grief had been absorbed by the hard Wyoming dirt years ago. His tears had dried up and blown away. Why should he care where she'd come from?

Well, he obviously did care, because here he was, riding in a tin bucket on the last leg of the trip to Piedras Island. Except for the vast amount of water surrounding him, the much lower altitude, and the crowds of cars and trucks on the highways, Washington so far wasn't that much different from Wyoming. At least there were mountains to look at. Not as breathtaking as the Tetons, but they were okay.

After calling the Barstow Police Department and talking to Detective Garcia, Dakota now knew his mother had been murdered not long after she'd left the ranch all those years ago. Maybe she'd meant to come back. He would never know, but he suspected not. She'd abandoned him. Left without leaving a note or message of any kind.

Tad had helpfully pointed out that if Dakota had gone with her, he probably would've ended up in foster care instead of on Tad's family's spread. Or dead. Maybe the guy had a point, but Dakota was allowed to be angry with her. Being murdered didn't let her off the hook.

Tad had "run into" Niall Hamarsson before he'd left Collier's Creek. Dakota totally suspected his friend had searched the man out. Thaddeus Wayne Gillespie was the reason Dakota was about to step foot on Piedras Island. Tad was a good friend who only wanted Dakota to be happy.

And it was possible that Dakota was a little curious about where Ana Green had come from. Hamarsson. Whatever. She'd never said anything about family, grandparents, or a brother. He didn't even know who his dad was, other than some guy whose last name was Green. Maybe.

Something caught his attention, and Dakota peered out at the water. His heart began to beat faster. Was that a seal floating out there? He squinted hard, trying to bring whatever it was into focus. No, what he'd seen was just a log bobbing up and down, dammit. If he had to travel to Washington State, he very much wanted to see a seal for the first time. A seal was one thing he wouldn't see at home. Disappointment had him slumping back in his seat.

As it had for the past ten days, his brain immediately circled back to the fact that he had a fucking older brother.

An. Older. *Brother*.

Even though he denied it to Tad, he'd seen the resemblance between himself and Niall Hamarsson. Dakota had also Googled the guy. He may have grown up outside of a tiny town in the middle of Wyoming, the state with the smallest population in the US, but he knew his way around the internet.

Niall Hamarsson had been a cop in Seattle. Now he was an investigator with some business called West Coast Forensics. Dakota had enlarged and stared at Niall's profile picture until he'd given himself a headache. It felt a little like looking into his future, or at a ghost from his past. He'd stared long and hard, trying to impose his mother's features on his brother's. It was hard since he didn't have any pictures of her.

The ferry bumped hard against something, snapping him out of his thoughts. Grabbing the table, Dakota froze, waiting for whatever was about to happen. Had they run aground? Could ferries do that? Was the boat sinking? But then a man's voice came on overhead saying it was time to disembark and he felt like a fool. He glanced around but didn't think anyone had seen his panic.

As he stood up, his cell phone vibrated. Pulling it out of his pocket, he glanced at the screen. It was Tad, of course. Who else would call him?

"What," Dakota said.

"Jeez." As always, Tad ignored the less than enthusiastic greeting. "Are you there yet? Did you make it all the way to the edge of the world?"

Dakota looked out the window again. From his vantage point, he could see some colorful buildings and what looked like a town about the size of Collier's Creek, plus lots of evergreen trees and more boats of all shapes and sizes than he'd ever seen before in his life.

"Yeah, the ferry just landed."

"I think it's docked," Tad teased.

"Docked," Dakota repeated, rolling his eyes. "I'm really here. Feels kind of surreal."

"Are you going to try and find him today?"

Him. Niall Hamarsson. Dakota took a deep breath and let it back out again.

It was that fine line between late afternoon and early evening. Dakota had been on the road for two days, living on anger and fast food, sleeping in his gas-guzzling ancient Ford Bronco in shopping mall parking lots and rest areas. If nothing else, he was ready for a bathroom with a shower.

"I think so."

"You should, just drive directly there. Look, Dakota, maybe try and get to know him, give him a chance? I know it's got to be hard."

"Says the guy whose family is something out of a fairy tale."

Yes, Dakota was jealous of Tad's family. It wasn't an emotion he was proud of.

"You know Mom and Dad love you like a son," Tad retorted. "Sometimes I think they love you more than me."

"Yeah, yeah."

Penny and Waylon Gillespie were kind people. Penny was constantly telling Dakota how proud she was of him and although Waylon was less effusive with his praise, he'd give Dakota a manful slap on the back every once in a while. They'd both been happy for him when he'd finally finished all his classes and even treated him to a celebratory dinner.

"So, you gonna go out there and just knock on his door?"

Before leaving Collier's Creek, Tad had insisted they look up Niall Hamarsson together. Tad wanted to know what Dakota's long-lost brother was all about. It hadn't been hard, seeing as how he'd left his business card. They'd already known he was an ex-homicide detective who now worked for some bigwig company that helped law enforcement with all sorts of cases, but they'd also learned that Hamarsson was gay and married.

That fact surprised Dakota. The two seconds he'd talked to him, the guy hadn't seemed gay, although Dakota knew how stupid that assumption was. He worked in relatively gay-friendly Collier's Creek and couldn't tell by a glance was a person's sexual orientation was. Dakota was bi, after all, and no one could tell just by looking at him either.

"Maybe. I guess."

Tad chuckled at his indecision. "Keep me updated."

"Okay. I've got to go now."

"Promise you'll call after."

"I promise."

Following the other passengers, Dakota jogged back down the metal staircase to his car, doing his best not to visualize somehow missing the ramp and driving off the ferry into the harbor. Tad's mom, Penny, had always told him he had an overactive imagination. Maybe he did, maybe he didn't. He just knew he didn't want to end up in the water.

Possibly, he mused, it would've been a good idea to let Hamarsson know he'd decided to come for the memorial. But Dakota hadn't wanted to commit to staying—or anything, really—before he stepped foot on the island where his mother had been born. Where she'd grown up.

The other thing Tad and Dakota had managed to figure out was where Hamarsson lived. On paper, the guy had a post office box. But Tad had the bright idea of looking at property records, and after scrutinizing the island, they'd found a parcel owned by Niall Hamarsson and Mat Dempsey.

If he felt brave enough, Dakota could be at the front door in twenty minutes or so.

Was he brave enough?

The car in front of him flashed its brake lights and started moving down the ramp. Dakota followed and seconds later, after a lot of clanging and banging and not falling into the water, he was finally on Piedras Island. The sun had set already, so there wasn't much to see except the lighted signs for various businesses on either side of the street.

Dakota's stomach growled, overriding his stupid nerves.

Ahead of him, someone pulled out of a parking spot directly in front of a place called The Hook. From the outside, it appeared to be one of those old-fashioned diners with hand-dipped milkshakes and gumball machines by the cash register like the Pioneer Café back home. The thought of a decent meal had him pulling over. If he was going to show up unannounced at Niall Hamarsson's house, he didn't want to do it on an empty stomach.

"YOU LOOK HUNGRY. What can I get you, sweetie?" The waitress asked. The name tag clipped to her shirt claimed her name was Grace.

Dakota glanced down at the menu in front of him even though he knew what he wanted. "Burger and fries, please."

He'd taken a seat at the counter, not wanting to take up a table. The place wasn't packed but there was a comfortable ambience to it. And they did have hand-dipped milkshakes.

"Good choice. Our shakes are world-famous," she added, continuing to smile at him.

"World-famous? Okay then, I'll have a chocolate shake too, thanks."

He was worried about his money lasting but his stomach overruled his brain. There would be extra hours to work at Jake's when he got back home. Maybe he could even start looking for a "real job" in Jackson or possibly there'd be an opening in Collier's Creek.

Grace cocked her head, looking at him closely. "I don't think I know you, but you seem awfully familiar."

"Oh, uh..." Dakota didn't know how to answer her.

Even Tad had commented how much Dakota and Niall resembled each other—except Hamarsson was darker-complected than Dakota. At the time, Dakota hadn't wanted to admit it out loud. But after spending way too much time staring at the older man's work picture, there was no way of getting around it. They were definitely related.

Did everyone on the island know Hamarsson? Was this going to happen everywhere he went?

Grace waved a hand nonchalantly. "Don't mind me, I'm just being silly. Everybody has a doppelgänger, right?" With that, she made a beeline for the pass-through behind the counter and clipped his order up.

While he waited for his food, Dakota watched the waitress bustle around and second-guessed everything he was doing— again. It wasn't as if coming to Piedras was going to bring his mother back, and he certainly didn't expect, or want, some big, happy family bullshit.

If nothing else, Ana had taught him to trust no one but himself. He'd been lucky when she'd ditched him in that she'd left him at Rolling Sky. Another place might have made him leave or put him in foster care. He'd been old enough to pull his own weight, and summers on a working ranch were busy. By the time the Gillespies had realized Dakota was still there and that Ana was nowhere to be found, Tad had basically imprinted himself on Dakota and refused to let him go.

So what if he'd forged a few signatures or let teachers think that Penny was his mom? It hadn't hurt anyone, and he'd fucking graduated on time.

A few minutes later, Grace slid the plate of food in front of him along with the milkshake.

"Enjoy, sweetheart. You look like you need a good meal."

LATER, when he was back behind the wheel of the Bronco, Dakota checked his cell phone again. There were no more calls from Tad. He considered texting that he was finally on his way but decided against it. He'd managed to waste forty-five minutes eating dinner—and the milkshake had been incredible—but it was time to get moving.

For fuck's sake, he'd driven the one thousand miles from Collier's Creek to Western Washington and then taken a damn boat across a huge amount of water.

He could fucking do this.

The drive to Hamarsson's place took him longer than he'd anticipated—Dakota missed the well-camouflaged driveway the first time he passed by it. But after a U-turn up the road, Dakota was turning left and bumping down a long gravel drive, his heart pounding against his ribs.

He briefly considered stopping and turning around, but it was already too late. The Bronco had passed through the stand of trees surrounding the property and the headlights lit up a newer-looking single-story wood house with two cars parked on the side, one an older Subaru and one a police cruiser with PCSD painted on the side.

"Crap."

He was at the right place.

Turning off the engine, he cracked open his door but didn't immediately step out. Once he knocked on that door, there really was no turning back. He stilled, hesitating, his fight and flight responses warring with each other. Flight was doing its best to win.

A light on the porch flicked on. Then a dog barked and he heard someone swear.

"Dammit, Fenrir."

Fuck. There was nowhere to hide.

The house beckoned him with its welcoming light and a promise of warmth, but Dakota reminded himself that he was angry. He tried to hold on to the emotion like a weapon, reminding himself that he was pissed off his life was being upended *again*. He hadn't asked for Niall Hamarsson to come strolling into his life. He'd never asked for a sibling. Not even a half brother.

Hamarsson hadn't given Dakota a choice about a memorial, had he? What if Dakota didn't want one? What if he just wanted to scream into the wind? Instead, he'd had to drive from Wyoming to Washington.

A light tap on the driver's side window scared the living crap out of him. Slowly turning his head, Dakota fully expected to see Niall Hamarsson standing there. He had no idea what to say. Instead, a different man waited next to the car.

He motioned for Dakota to either get out or roll his window down. His eyes were kind, different from Niall Hamarsson's and Dakota's. From his research, he recognized the county sheriff who was also Niall's husband, although he looked different out of his uniform.

With his thirtieth deep breath of the day, Dakota pushed the door all the way open and got out of the car, stretching to his full height. He was taller than Mat Dempsey by a few inches, but Dempsey appeared to be a wall of solid muscle whereas Dakota had trouble keeping weight on.

"Dakota Green, I presume? I'm Mat Dempsey," Dempsey said. "Come on inside. I promise the wolf doesn't bite although the cat sometimes does. No guarantees about Niall."

"Wolf?"

"I'm joking, although Fenrir is part wolfhound. Don't be shy, you've traveled this far. Sorry for startling you. I was outside already when you pulled in."

Turning away, Mat started toward the house, seeming to expect that Dakota would follow him.

Huh.

Slamming the Bronco door shut, Dakota did exactly that,

shaking his head as he stomped across the lumpy grass. Did people just *follow* Dempsey like he was the pied fucking piper?

The front door opened when they stepped onto the porch deck. A hulking form Dakota recognized as Niall Hamarsson was silhouetted by the cabin's interior lights.

Niall fucking Hamarsson.

His only living relative—that Dakota knew of. That nugget of information had been rolling around in Dakota's head like a rock in his boot since Hamarsson had shown up in Collier's Creek. Dakota didn't know what to do with a brother. After a year, he'd known his mom wasn't coming back, and it was Dakota Green against the world. No one to answer to, but also no one to fall back on. Except Tad. Tad was a constant.

But all that time, there'd been a brother out there.

"Dakota," Niall said, stepping back to let them both inside. "I wasn't sure you'd make it." A large, shaggy, gray dog pushed past Niall to sniff at Dakota's legs. "Come inside."

"Don't mind Fenrir," Dempsey added as he shut the door behind them. "He's just figuring out where you've been."

Dakota stepped past Niall, appreciating that the man didn't offer to shake his hand.

The house's open-plan interior reminded Dakota a little of Tad's parents' home, only much smaller. He was standing in what was the kitchen-living room area and down a short hallway saw other doors that presumably led to bedrooms and a bathroom.

"Tad convinced me I should come," Dakota said, stopping by what looked to be their dining table. "We're not going to be best friends or anything, just to be clear."

From behind him, Dempsey coughed, and Niall shot him an indecipherable look over Dakota's shoulder. He followed up his glance with a shrug and moved over to the refrigerator.

"Are you going to take your coat off and stick around long enough for a beer," Niall asked, "or dinner if you're hungry?"

Dakota could almost hear Penny's voice reminding him to be polite. That it wasn't either of their faults that they were in an awkward situation.

"I ate at a café in town called The Hook," he said, taking off his hat and looking around for where to hang it. "But a beer would be good."

"Here." Mat held his hand out. "We just pile them on the hooks over by the door."

Dakota hesitated before lifting a hand and unbuttoning his heavy coat. Taking the jacket from him, Mat hung it by the door. It blended in with their collection of slickers, parkas, and lightweight outerwear.

Niall held out a can of beer. "Maybe not as good as at Jake's Tap, but it's pretty decent."

Popping the seal on his beer, Niall lifted it upward.

"Here's to weird shit."

"Niall," Mat groaned.

"He's right," Dakota said, lifting his own still-sealed can. "Here's to weird fucking shit."

Maybe Tad was right and this visit wouldn't be horrible. Dakota vowed not to tell him—he'd never hear the end of it.

MAT

Oh, hell yes.

Mat hid his laugh with a cough as he ran his fingers along the top of Fenrir's head so Niall wouldn't see. When he stood up again, Niall shot him a look that, if Mat were a fearful man, might have had him running for the hills. Luckily, Niall didn't intimidate Mat and neither did this baby-Niall.

Niall had told him that he and Dakota Green looked alike but he hadn't mentioned just how similar they were in both looks and personality. It was going to be fun to be on the sidelines watching while they circled each other, growling like feral cats. His mom was right again. It didn't take a genius to see that Dakota Green was a lonely, hurting young man.

"I'll take a beer too. One of those red ales," he said to Niall.

Shooting another narrow-eyed glance, Niall grabbed Mat a beer from the fridge and handed it to him. After Niall's toast, both Hamarsson men remained stubbornly silent. If this kept up, they would never get to know each other. Apparently, Mat got to be on the sidelines as a referee.

"How was the drive out here, Dakota?" Mat asked. "Have a seat."

He took his normal seat at their table, motioning for Dakota to sit down as well. Niall turned back to one of the kitchen cupboards, presumably rummaging around for three glasses.

"It was fine."

Mat mentally rolled his eyes up to the ceiling.

"Do you have a place to stay?" he asked.

Dakota shook his head. "I'll sleep in my car." His words were clipped but Mat could hear a slight drawl.

Mat met Niall's dark gaze from across the room, and he shook his head ever so slightly. Mat agreed. Dakota sleeping in his car wasn't going to happen. The kid was a fresh feral though. Was it going to be killing him with kindness? Or reverse psychology?

"You're more than welcome here but if you want a little more space, my mom also has a spare room. As sheriff, I can't let you sleep in your car." Complete crap but maybe the kid would believe him.

Dakota's equally dark gaze skated past Mat to Niall and finally down to the dog, who'd completed his investigation of Dakota and was now leaning against his thigh. Mat wasn't surprised by this. Fenrir seemed to smile and rested his head on Dakota's lap.

"Fenrir, go to your bed," Mat said.

Fenrir, no surprise to Mat or Niall, did not budge.

"It's okay," Dakota said quietly, looking down at the best psychologist in the room.

"What Mat's not telling you is that his mom, Alyson, is a human lie detector," Niall said as he set down three mismatched glasses on the table and sat down across from Mat and next to Dakota. "Actually, that's not right. She's a truth machine. She'll have you spilling deep, dark secrets that you didn't even know about yourself. If you're willing to risk it, however, she's also a great cook. But Fenrir stays here."

Dakota's attention bounced back and forth between the three of them but he didn't say anything. Mat did notice that his fingers shook as he popped open the beer and poured it into his glass.

Mat took a long drink and set his glass back down. "Niall says you work at a brewery in Collier's Creek?"

"Yeah," Dakota answered shortly. Raising his glass to his lips, Dakota took a big, almost defiant, gulp of beer. Setting it down with a thud, he returned to stroking the dog's head. "For now."

Mat glanced at Niall again. The kid was not on Piedras to talk about beer or to pet the dog. Although Fenrir's opinion was likely different. They needed to quit dancing around the real issue because ignoring why Dakota was sitting at their table would not change the past.

"It must have been a surprise when Niall showed up," Mat said. "A hell of a way to learn about your mom. I'm truly sorry, Dakota."

"Yeah." He paused, and Mat thought he was going to leave it at that, but then he continued, focusing on his glass instead of Mat or Niall. "I figured something bad had happened."

"We did too," Mat agreed somberly.

"You told Tad she left you too." It was the first time he'd directly addressed Niall.

It was so hard for Mat to watch Dakota, to watch the complicated emotions crowding him. What had the kid done to survive? How had he not ended up in the care system?

"When I was six or so," Niall agreed. "But, like I told your friend, my—*our*—grandparents found out eventually and took me in. Look," he continued, pursing his lips, "I should've sent a letter instead of ambushing you at your work, and for that, I apologize." Dakota shrugged again. At this rate, he was going to wear his shoulders out. "Notification of kin is one of the hardest things we do."

To that statement, Dakota's expression changed slightly, still suspicious but also thoughtful.

"Is that why you're a cop?" he asked Niall.

"I'm not a cop anymore, but to answer your question, yes, Ana's disappearance was a major factor in my career path."

"Huh." His questioning gaze slid over to Mat. Dakota had done his research.

"My dad was sheriff here on Piedras. I was a cop in San Francisco before I came back home."

"And now you're the sheriff."

"Yep. Bossing people around, giving tickets to trespassers and unruly teenagers. I'm definitely living the high life."

"Don't listen to him," Niall said. "He loves it."

"Really?"

"Really," agreed Mat.

All three of them were quiet again. The wind started blowing outside, making the trees creak. It was March, rain was probably in the forecast.

"So," Niall said, standing up from the table, "are you staying with us or are you willing to risk Alyson—Mat's mom? Mat has to be up and out early but unless there's a staff meeting, I generally work from here. Here you'll get peace and quiet and decent coffee. At Alyson's, you'll be nagged into sharing your life story but the payoff is good food."

"You could take him to Mom's for lunch tomorrow," Mat pointed out. "Probably she's a bit much after a long drive and sitting down with a half brother you only found out about a week ago."

"Yeah, alright, but it's up to Dakota."

They both looked at him expectantly.

"I'll stay here, I guess."

Mat repressed a snicker. Dakota's attitude would change. He just needed to let Piedras seep into his being. Mat doubted his default personality was bubbly, but he'd inherited a healthy dose of the natural Hamarsson reticence.

"SIR."

"Chief Deputy?"

Birdy shook her head at him.

"We got the cell phone records for Arsen Hollis."

"Finally!" Mat didn't bother taking off his jacket; instead, he headed straight to Birdy's desk. "Anything interesting?"

"I just started to go through them. He appears to have spent a lot of time on the phone."

"Makes sense since he was a realtor. Start with the frequently called numbers so we can rule them out."

There was a silence and Mat looked from the monitor back to Birdy.

"Right. You've got this. Okay, then. I'll go about my day. I'm going to take a lunch hour today, can you cover?"

"Of course I can, sir."

"Knock it off with the sir business. I'm sorry I implied you needed direction. I'm distracted because I just left Niall and mini-Niall at home alone." He headed over to his desk as he spoke.

"Oh?"

"The half brother he met in Wyoming showed up last night. Dakota's here for the memorial Saturday. Birdy, he is so much like Niall."

"That could be... interesting?"

Mat appreciated Birdy's skepticism. She knew Niall well,

almost as well as Mat did. Thus, she had a pretty good idea of Dakota and she hadn't met him yet.

"Right? They could *not* talk each other's ears off." Taking his coat off, Mat hung it on the back of his chair. "They could sit in the same house and not communicate *all day long*. I'll go home for lunch and neither of them will have said a damn word."

"You're going home for lunch why, sir?"

"Someone has to poke them, make them talk. Before I left this morning, I dug out the only photo album Niall has with pictures of Od and Jo and left it on the table." He grinned. "I also texted Ryder."

"Ryder?" Birdy narrowed her eyes as she tried to figure out why Mat would let Ryder know that Dakota Green was in town. Comprehension dawned. "Oh, you want him to help break the ice between Niall and his brother?"

Mat nodded, tapping his mouse so his desktop powered on. "And he'll tell Shay. Shay might not be genetically related to Dakota, but as Niall's other half brother, he might have some perspective. Plus, he's nicer than Niall."

By the time the other on-duty deputies had straggled into the office, Mat and Birdy had narrowed the list of phone numbers down to twelve that needed to be called and verified. One of the numbers Hollis had called or texted over twenty times in the month before his death.

"That's gonna be the one," Mat said. "That number will lead us to the perp."

Birdy frowned as she also stared at the sheet. "But Hollis was a real estate agent. Couldn't that number belong to a client?"

Mat pointed at their printout. "I doubt he was talking to a client after ten at night. Maybe one time, if they were in the middle of negotiations or something, but not nine. These were booty calls."

"Booty call?" Birdy repeated, giving him a sideways look and wrinkling her nose. "Really?"

"From what Stone told us, Hollis didn't do committed relationships. Therefore, booty calls."

"Gross."

"Flip you for the calls?" Mat waggled his eyebrows.

Birdy just rolled her eyes and slid the list toward herself. "I'll do them. You head out and check on Mrs. Johnson. You know she prefers you to me."

"It's the Dempsey charm."

"It's something anyway."

AFTER HE'D CHECKED in on Mrs. Johnson and had a brownie, responded to a one-car accident with no injuries—just a freaked-out teenager who'd swerved to avoid a squirrel—and driven all the way out to English Park for good measure, Mat pointed his cruiser toward home. He'd valiantly resisted calling or texting to check in with Niall to see how things were going.

As he'd predicted last night, a storm had blown in and now thick clouds were lingering over the island, snared by the tops of the tallest cedars. Everything was damp. Heading back through Killegan's Point, Mat spotted a pair of runners in matching high-vis vests jogging along the shoulder just past Chester's Grocery. This wasn't the kind of weather Mat liked to go for a run in, but there was always some nut willing to brave the yuck.

"Nope, not gonna happen," he muttered.

Something in his brain pinged at him, demanding his attention. Glancing in his rearview mirror, he tried to figure out what his subconscious had picked up on, but no luck. Slowing down, he did a quick U-turn and headed back, passing the joggers again and driving until he'd reached Chester's parking lot. It was useless though; whatever he'd noticed had slipped back into the murky depths of his mind. The harder he tried to pull it up, the further it slipped away.

"Dammit," he growled, gripping the steering wheel tighter. He hated when that happened. It—whatever *it* was—was going to bug him the rest of the day.

"HEY," Mat said, doing his best to shake off the feeling he'd missed something important as he came in through the front door.

Niall occupied his usual spot at the kitchen table. As a bonus, he was wearing his newish reading glasses, which Mat found far too sexy. If they hadn't had a house guest, he might have done something about it.

"Hey," Niall replied, taking the glasses off and setting them next to his laptop.

Technically, they were both on the clock and Dakota was lurking, Mat reminded himself. Unzipping his jacket, Mat shrugged it off and hung it up with the rest of them. He turned toward the fridge before remembering they'd talked about Alyson's. However, Mat had forgotten to call and ask. Another surge of irritation threatened to wash over him.

"Where's Dakota?"

Mini-Niall was around somewhere. Mat had seen his beat-to-hell Ford Bronco parked in the same spot from last night. With his arms folded across his chest, Mat leaned back against the kitchen counter. Seeming to appear out of nowhere, Hel jumped up and began rubbing her face against Mat's shoulder.

"You're not supposed to be up here," he reminded her. Picking her up, he held her close, enjoying the rumble of her purr. Fenrir was her dog, but Mat was her human.

"Dakota took a walk and Fenrir went along. Hel feels sorry for herself even though she could have gone with them."

"She hasn't warmed up to Dakota yet?"

Niall shook his head. Hel was a funny little cat, one that was very stingy with her affection. She squirmed out of Mat's arms and clambered up to sit on his shoulder.

"How's it been this morning?" Mat asked.

"Fine."

When he didn't say anything else, Mat glared at his husband.

"What?" Niall protested, his voice rising. "It's *fine*. Things have been *fine*. I've been working. Dakota had some coffee, flipped through that photo album you left out, then went for a walk. Ryder texted but I told him to stick his nose back out of my business and promised him we'd meet for lunch today. Things are fine."

"Fine is a word I hate." Hel bumped her wet nose against his ear.

"Sorry, I don't have a better word." Niall glanced at his watch. "He's been gone a while. He should be back soon."

"I forgot to call Mom and ask about lunch. We finally got Hollis's cell phone records."

"I talked to Alyson already. She's planning something for tomorrow. We'll go to the Brooch today and that way we can talk to Sage and Cody about Saturday. A whole flock of birds and one stone." Niall rose to his feet. "Maybe that will make him feel more comfortable on Saturday. Did you learn anything interesting from the records?"

"Not really. There are a few numbers he called often. Birdy is taking care of the list."

"You seem... irritated."

"I am." He rolled his shoulders and Hel jumped down with a huff and stalked off toward their bedroom. "On my way here I noticed something but I can't figure out what it was. You know what I mean? When your brain sees something but doesn't tell you why it matters? I've been trying to figure it out ever since."

"What did it make you think of?"

"The Hollis case, but I was already thinking about it. That's all I've been thinking about."

"Where were you?"

Mat appreciated that Niall was just trying to help, but it wasn't as if he hadn't spent the last ten minutes wracking his brain about it.

"Chester's, or around there," he answered, throwing his hands up in frustration. "It's like an itch in the middle of my back that I can't reach. Who knows? It could've been something when I was out at the park or from when I drove by the mobile home park—anywhere. Who the fuck knows?"

"Hmm." A lazy expression Mat recognized well slowly bloomed on Niall's face. A little smile teased his lips. "I like it when you get all fired up. Normally you're so even-keeled. Maybe I should scratch that itch for you."

The smile turned predatory. Niall edged closer to Mat, forcing him to back up against the countertop. Their torsos touched and Mat could feel the thump-thump of Niall's heart.

"Niall." Mat attempted to infuse the word with irritation but it sounded more like a plea. Especially since he'd been having similar thoughts when he walked in the door.

A thump on the porch had Niall scowling and stepping away from him. Dakota and Fenrir had returned.

Niall shot an aggravated glance toward the front door, wishing that Mat had come home earlier or his half brother had stayed out longer. The bumping was followed by the doorknob turning and the damn door opening. Fenrir trotted inside, his tail high, followed by Dakota. The salty scent of the strait came inside with them.

"How was it down there?" Niall asked, stepping further away from Mat.

"Fine."

Mat stared at their guest, waiting for more information.

"Windy," Dakota added.

"It's always windy here," Mat agreed.

"I'm used to it."

A four-word sentence from Dakota was a record. Niall was beginning to appreciate that being naturally reticent could be irritating for other people. But also fuck 'em if they didn't want to make an effort.

"Did you get a hold of your friend?" Niall asked, making an effort because he needed to. His half brother had made the effort, driving all the way to Piedras. He was a stranger and Niall... needed to try and get to know him.

"Yeah," Dakota replied.

Niall thought he was going to leave it at that but then he added, "Tad was at work. We talked for a couple minutes."

Niall glanced over at Mat, hoping for an assist, but Mat had grabbed a towel and was rubbing Fenrir down. Fenrir had a love-hate relationship with the towel and either reveled in the rubdown or did his best to dismember the thick fabric. Today he was enjoying being dried off.

Mat was home but Niall was on his own.

"TAD SEEMED like an alright guy when I met him."

Dakota brightened almost imperceptibly. "He's a good person. We've known each other since we were kids."

Niall thought he'd been about to add something more but stopped himself.

"Are you hungry, Dakota?" Niall knew he wasn't the best host. He'd made a pot of coffee, but he was rarely hungry much before noon. "We were thinking of taking you to lunch at the Brooch, where the memorial will be on Saturday. Then, after Mat goes back to work, you and I can go over some details."

"Okay." Dakota's eyes narrowed and he glanced back and forth between Mat and Niall. "But I'll pay for my own meal."

Niall looked over at Mat again. His husband's shoulders were shaking, and it wasn't because of the dog's antics. Asshole.

"Look, Dakota," Niall began. Dakota turned his head to look at him. "This isn't fucking charity, or me trying to get on your good side. This is me being nice and, admittedly, not wanting to cook. And let me tell you, me being nice is a rare fucking occurrence. Ask anyone, ask Mat if you want to. Believe me, I know this, this situation, it's difficult. It's difficult for me too."

Straightening to his full height and facing both of them, Mat opened his mouth to say something, but Dakota got there first.

"This is just." He shrugged. "I don't know anything, and this place isn't my family or my home. Maybe I should just go back to Wyoming."

"First of all," Mat started before Niall could mess things up even more, "like it or not, Dakota, you do suddenly have family. So much damn family. You'll even meet some of them today if you come to lunch. And you'll meet the rest on Saturday. This island is crazy with family. You won't be genetically related to all of them, but they will accept you with open arms—even if you're not the hugging type. Furthermore, Niall isn't nice. But he is loyal, almost to a fault. When you finally get past that Hamarsson exterior, I think you'll find"— he cut himself off and Niall was sure he'd been about to say they were alike, but instead he ended with—"this is hard for Niall too."

He and Dakota stared at each other. Dakota shifted his stance, crossing his arms over his chest, and Niall caught himself before he did the same. Ooh, boy.

Fine. Yes. He and Dakota had similarities. Poor Mat.

"Not to put too fine a point on it, but maybe put yourself in Niall's shoes," Mat continued. "Ana abandoned him on a city street and he lived in foster care for months. He never saw her again after that. Then forty years later, he finds out she had another child and seemingly was happy enough—for a while. Niall never saw Ana happy."

"Not quite forty, come on," Niall complained.

"I'm not finished."

"I didn't know any of this," admitted Dakota.

Because Niall hadn't said anything, and Dakota hadn't asked.

"Because you and Niall are the two most stubborn people I've ever met! I left the photo album out so you would have something to talk about but instead... gah!" Snapping his mouth shut, Mat threw up his hands in frustration and glared at both of them.

Niall caught Dakota's wide-eyed glance and quirked an eyebrow ever so slightly.

"Maybe we should make an attempt to get to know each other. What do you say?"

"I guess," Dakota said, a hint of laughter in his tone.

In that moment, Niall knew things were going to be all right, eventually. It wasn't going to be easy, but there was hope.

"So, lunch?" Niall asked. "Unless you have something more to add, Mat? Moral failings? The fact that I sometimes forget to rinse the sink after I shave?"

Dakota's stomach betrayed him, rumbling at Niall's suggestion they eat. He nodded. "I could eat something."

NIALL TOOK the Subaru with Dakota in the passenger seat and Mat followed them in his cruiser. He'd even remembered to text Sage and Cody, warning—letting them know—that they were coming for lunch. The notice was equally for Dakota and himself. He and Dakota were going to have to stay after Mat left and talk details. They didn't need to be overwhelmed by a bunch of people showing up all at once.

Shay and Ryder were joining them—when Niall had managed to head Ryder off from showing up at the cabin earlier, he'd promised that he'd introduce Dakota at lunch—and not at Alyson's either. It was a good thing Dakota had agreed to come along. And damn Mat Dempsey for his loving interference.

"So," Niall said over the rumble of the tires and swish of the windshield wipers, "Brooch Resort is locally owned and has been around since the early 1900s in one form or another. The current owner is Cody Prescott. He's a friend of ours. Cody can be... a lot. But his heart is in the right place."

How to describe Cody to someone who hadn't met him?

Cody and Ryder were similar, and it wasn't just because of their ages. Cody often appeared to have an undiagnosed case of ADHD in search of medication. Ryder was enthusiastic and energetic and could talk the paint off a wall, but he was focused and had an incredible memory. Cody was focused and talented too, he just camouflaged his strengths so that folks often underestimated him. To their detriment. The Brooch was flourishing under his management.

"Just know that Cody and my coworker, Ryder, are excited to meet you. Don't let their weird cheerfulness get to you, I swear it's natural. They aren't related to us."

There was a sound from Niall's right that he could have sworn was a chuckle.

"Okay, noted."

"Ryder and I work together so I can tell him to shut it."

Another louder chuckle.

"We'll meet with Sage and Cody after we eat. And god knows who else, but she warned me that I—*we*—need to decide how we want this to go on Saturday. Do we want to speak? Personally, I'm going to let others do the talking seeing as how I don't have very good memories of Ana, but maybe you have something you'd like to share."

"I don't know yet. I don't think I want to say anything."

"People are going to be curious about you," Niall warned. "You can take a leaf out of the Hamarsson book and tell them to fuck off if you want. I'll back you up."

Now Niall regretted not talking to Dakota this morning about the photos Mat'd gotten out, and about life in general. But he'd stayed in the guest room until after Mat left for the station and only emerged when Niall had tapped on his door to let him know there was coffee.

"Tad thinks I should say something."

"Tad seemed like a smart guy. Maybe he's got the right idea."

Niall figured Tad was the main reason Dakota had come to Piedras. After talking to him outside the bed-and-breakfast, Tad had promised Niall he would do his best to convince Dakota to make the trip, and he'd been true to his word.

"But it's okay not to speak. You don't owe the people here anything." Dakota didn't owe Ana anything, either.

They were passing through Killegan's Point now and Niall pressed on the brake pedal, figuring Dakota might want to see the sights, such as they were. Chester's was still pink and gray—it looked about time for a clearance sale repainting. Next door, through the laundromat's grimy window, Niall saw someone sitting in a chair, doing something on their phone while waiting for their laundry. The hardware store sign had been freshly painted and a rolling rack of colorful perennials sat out front.

"The other town on the island," Niall said. "Killegan's Point."

Dakota stayed quiet and Niall realized his jaw hurt from tensing it. Small talk was not something he excelled at. Hell, if there was an exam for it, Niall would've failed.

"What does Tad think you should say about Ana?"

He thought that Dakota might ignore the question so he was surprised when Dakota spoke after another short silence.

"She made good ebelskivers."

"She did?"

He'd forgotten about ebelskivers. Niall didn't remember Ana cooking for him, not once. In his memories from back then, they'd lived in her friends' spare rooms, sometimes living rooms, often sleeping on couches. Not places conducive to much culinary creativity. Ebelskivers were something their grandmother had made on special occasions. They may have originated in Denmark but the very Norwegian Jo Hamarsson had co-opted them for her family. They weren't good for you, being fried pocket mini pancakes stuffed with jam and liberally doused with powdered sugar. He could almost taste the sweet treats and he hadn't had one in years. Maybe Alyson could be convinced to make them.

"Yeah. She made them for my birthday sometimes."

Niall wanted to know how old Dakota was when Ana had disappeared. Instead, he asked, "When's your birthday?"

"Don't you know all about me from the paperwork?"

A smile threatened to curve Niall's lips. Dakota was smart too.

"Yeah, but pretend I forgot." He had, in fact, forgotten.

"June ninth."

Thank god they were approaching the turn for the Brooch.

"Here we are," he announced, veering right into the resort's parking area. After coasting into an open spot not too far from the front entrance, he set the parking brake and turned off the engine. Silence filled the cab. It wasn't an uncomfortable quiet, just... quiet.

Mat pulled in and parked on Niall's side of the car. Niall glanced out his window, meeting his questioning gaze, and shrugged. *I'm trying*, he mouthed. Even through two panes of glass, Niall clearly saw the skeptical expression paired with an eye roll. Niall raised a finger and flipped him off.

Returning his attention to his passenger, Niall saw Dakota was peering at the ornate four-story building with balconies on the upper-level suites and long black hooks sunk high into the walls, hooks that would hold enormous planters filled with impatiens, petunias, and other flowers Niall couldn't name later in the season. The work Cody and his partner, Wade Buckner, had done in the past couple of years was paying off. The resort was gorgeous, with fresh paint and repaired balconies. A separate building that had burned was rebuilt and they now served the best pizza in all the islands.

Niall cracked his door open. "Let's go."

WITH MAT by his side and Dakota trailing slightly behind them, Niall led the way across the parking lot to the more casual pub. The Kiln was a favorite place of Niall's. He enjoyed being somewhat anonymous under its dim lighting and shadowy corners. Midweek the restaurant was about half full. March wasn't a busy time of year but things were starting to pick up.

With a half wave to Ona, the daytime server, Niall spotted a large round table in one of the darker corners and headed toward it. With luck, no one uninvited would come over to greet them. But since everyone on the island liked Sheriff Dempsey, that was probably a lost cause. Mat carried a light that was all his own. As selfish as he was, Niall knew he couldn't keep it all for himself.

"Do you already know what you'd like to drink?" Ona asked them as she dropped three menus on the table. "Hey, Sheriff, it's been a while since you stopped in."

"Coffee for me," said Mat. "You know how it is, I've been busy sheriffing."

Ona laughed and turned to Niall and Dakota.

To Niall's surprise, Dakota took the seat next to his.

"Coffee for me. We're meeting with Cody after this. And two more menus for Ryder and Shay."

"Just water," said Dakota. Ona shot him an inquiring look. To her credit, she didn't overtly stare, but Niall noticed her glance between them. He suspected they'd be getting a lot of that while Dakota was on the island.

From his position facing the door, Niall was the first to see that Shay and Ryder had arrived. Ryder spotted them immediately and started toward them.

"Incoming," Niall muttered.

"Admit it, you love Ryder," Mat said.

"I'm not admitting anything."

Niall did like Ryder Mann, but no way was he admitting it out loud when Ryder was close enough to hear him.

"Hi, everyone," Ryder said, plopping down on the other side of Mat.

Shay took the seat next to his husband, leaving a space between himself and Dakota. He picked up one of the menus and began reading it.

"What's the special today, did you guys find out?" Shay looked over the cardstock, then at Dakota. "You must be Dakota. I'm Shay Delacombe, Niall's other half brother, and this is my husband, Ryder Mann." With that, he went back to perusing his lunch choices.

"Hi, Dakota," Ryder said. "I work with Niall, but I'm sure he told you that."

"He did," Dakota acknowledged.

"Ryder." Shay elbowed his partner warningly.

"What? I just want to get to know Dakota. It can't have been easy for him to come all the way here not knowing anyone. If it were me, I would want to know everything. Feel free to ask me anything."

"Thankfully, not everyone is you, Ryder," Niall said dryly. "Maybe he'd just like to enjoy his meal instead of a round of Twenty Questions."

Before Ryder could start with his interrogation, Ona returned. "What can I get for you today?"

When Ona had retreated with their food order, Dakota asked, "How did you get into police work, Ryder?"

Niall knew the story, they all did, but he was curious how the younger man would answer the question.

"Well, it's a long story and wasn't entirely legal, so we'll skip that part. But the short story is that my mom went missing when I was a kid and was never found. After college, I started working for West Coast Forensics and haven't looked back."

"I believe it was a 'using his powers for good and not evil' situation," Shay added with a smirk at his husband.

"Potato and all that," Ryder agreed. "I love what we do. It's not glamorous like TV or anything, and investigations take a long time from beginning to end, but it's totally worth it. Are you interested in law enforcement?"

"I just graduated from a criminal justice program in Wyoming," Dakota said. "Right now, I'm working at a pub, but I'm hoping to get on at the sheriff's department in Collier's Creek or maybe Jackson."

Mat elbowed Niall in the ribs.

"What was that for?" he demanded indignantly.

"You know exactly what it's for," Mat said with a laugh.

"It's in your blood! Or not," Ryder muttered. "It's in something anyway. You and Niall seem to have a lot in common."

"Huh, and funny how we didn't know this until now," Mat muttered.

"Ryder," Niall said, narrowing his eyes at his coworker, "shut it."

"You don't scare me, Mr. Cranky Pants," Ryder said, shaking his menu at Niall.

Next to Niall, Dakota stifled a chuckle and his shoulders shook. Niall met Shay's amused glance. Not even Niall Hamarsson could keep Ryder down.

· · ·

THEIR FOOD ARRIVED and Mat and Ryder carried the lunch conversation, deftly avoiding the reason they were all there by talking about island things. In Mat's case, it was the county budget. In Ryder's, it was his obsession with Jewel Dairy ice cream and how he was trying to talk Benny into naming the next flavor *Frannie's Fraise Spectaculaire.*

"Frannie's fraise spectaculaire?" Dakota asked. "What even is that?"

"Frannie is one of Benny's goats. She's my favorite," Ryder explained.

Dakota just looked perplexed.

"Jewel Dairy? Have you not tried any of their ice cream yet?" Ryder looked between Niall and Dakota. Niall shrugged. Ice cream was not his thing.

"Ryder, he's only been here since last night," Niall pointed out.

"You should try some while you're here," Mat said, clearly a member of the same fan club as Ryder. "Although I'm not sure about goat milk ice cream."

"Believe me," Ryder said, his eyes wide, "it's so good. Meet up with me tomorrow and we'll go together."

"Ryder, you also like pineapple on pizza," Shay pointed out, "and me, so your life choices are questionable."

Ryder looked thoughtful, tapping his lip. "So, are you the pizza, or the pineapple?"

Luckily for them all, Mat's phone buzzed and there was no time for Shay to answer. From the way Mat immediately stood from his chair and vaguely waved goodbye while making his way out the door, his phone pressed to his ear, Niall figured the call might be about the Hollis case.

Shay finished his last bite and sat back in his chair. "Where are we meeting up with Sage and Cody? Here?"

Niall appreciated that Shay was joining them. Shay was

officially a good friend these days. Granted, it was Shay who'd been persistent, reaching out to Niall and inviting him and Mat for dinner and whatnot until Niall had given in. Mat often said Niall was feral and Niall had to agree.

"In the smaller conference room," Niall said. "We should head over now." He was ready to get the shitty part of the day over with.

MAT

"Yep," Birdy confirmed as Mat slid behind the wheel, his phone still at his ear. "Rick Peterson does not and never has worked for the Washington State ferry system."

"What the... How did the crew not know this when we were interviewing them?" Mat demanded.

"Well, sir, apparently there are a lot of new people and transfers who come over from other routes just so the ferry can operate on any given day. Peterson seems to have just joined the crew, acting like he belonged there. He wore the right clothing, had the orange vest. He fit right in. It was pure luck that I was comparing the list we got on the day of the murder to the official list the state finally sent over. We have one extra on ours."

The orange vest had been a way to hide in plain sight.

The truth hit Mat like a damn hammer. When he'd seen the joggers the other day, his brain had tried to suggest something, but he hadn't been able to get a grasp on it. High visibility vests stood out—and made faces harder to recall.

"Dammit. He could be anywhere now."

Mat started the engine and reversed out of the parking spot, fuming that the perp had pulled one over on them. The likelihood of catching up with Peterson now was almost zero. Less than zero. He'd disappeared into thin air and would only be caught if he walked into the station and confessed.

"Sir?"

Mat realized he'd never disconnected the call. He'd just set the thing in the console and possied up. Could one man be a posse? Mat decided the answer was yes, but he also had Birdy and the rest of the deputies, so they definitely had a posse, just not all the time.

Luckily, the early afternoon roads were traffic-free. He didn't need the lights to get around other drivers, although he flipped them on anyway to warn folks he was driving faster than he should on the slightly slick roads.

This was the first decent lead they'd had and even if Arsen Hollis didn't seem like a nice person in life, he didn't deserve to be shot in the head and left on the ferry deck. Mat did not approve of murder on his turf.

"Sir!" Birdy's voice was much louder and her tone sharper.

"Yes, Deputy?" He used deputy to remind himself who was supposed to be in charge. It never worked because Birdy was a natural leader no matter where she stood in line.

"I think Rick Peterson *is* his real name. Richard Michael Peterson."

Mat pulled over into the Chester's Grocery parking lot, letting the cruiser's engine idle while he processed this information.

"Say again?"

"We looked at all the IDs when the crew gave their statements and I think Rick Peterson's was authentic. I think he showed us his real driver's license."

"Why are criminals so stupid?"

"Can't answer that one, sir."

"Hold on, I'm less than five minutes away."

.   .   .

"MY THINKING, SIR," Birdy said when Mat rushed in through the front doors, "is that he panicked and didn't think about the possibility he would need a fake ID. I mean, he could've even said that he'd left his wallet at home or that it was in his car in Anacortes, but instead, he showed it to us. Maybe he thought he'd be able to get off the boat before the police arrived, but he messed up and was still there when we got there?"

Mat plopped down in his squeaky desk chair and spun to face her.

"And?"

"And," Birdy said smugly, "his listed address is in Lacey."

Lacey was a small community just north of Olympia. Not far from Hollis's address at all.

"Ugh." They were going to have to ask the Lacey Police Department for help. They were likely as short-staffed as Mat was. What would really happen was that one of them would have to make the trip down to Lacey.

"And"—if possible, his chief deputy's expression became smugger—"it seems he has a connection here on Piedras. Richard Michael Peterson is listed as owning a property in Killegan's Point. Looks like he inherited it. There's a quit claim deed in the county records associated with it, and the prior owner, Connie Peterson, appears to have passed away several years ago. We should check there before heading to Lacey."

Had he known Connie Peterson? Mat wasn't sure. The person to ask would be his mother. Alyson kept her finger on the pulse of Piedras and what she didn't know Stu Dennis did.

"Agreed. Anything for less legwork. But seriously, Birdy, why would he still be on the island?"

Birdy shrugged. "Like you asked, why are criminals so

stupid? Maybe since it's been over a week, he thinks he got away with it?"

"Or he doesn't have anything to do with Hollis's death," said Mat. "We need to keep that in mind."

Birdy bit her lip. "I suppose it's possible."

Mat squinted at the driver's license photo Birdy had pulled up on her screen. At the time the picture was taken, Peterson had a heavy beard, like the ones that seemed pretty popular these days. Mat tried to match the face with the crew he recalled interviewing and couldn't. All he could visualize was a sea of orange vests.

"I think he's shaved off the beard," he said. "He doesn't seem familiar. I don't think I've interacted with him here on the island. Although that picture is almost ten years old, he could have changed."

"What's the plan?"

"Let's see if there's anything else we can dig up on him before we head out there to question him. It would be great if we could do this without spooking him. I want to be as certain as we can that this is our guy."

"Could be the wrong man," Birdy said, her tone bitter. "Could randomly be some other Rick Peterson who owns property on the island and is the same age as the Rick Peterson who doesn't work for the Washington State ferry system."

"Did you and Leo have a fight?"

"No." She frowned at him. "I'm just mad he's been under our noses this whole time."

"Well, he still could have left. The ferry isn't the only way on or off this island."

Birdy stared at the screen as if the man in the picture would start speaking to her.

"I don't think so, sir. I think he's here. I think he never updated his address with the state."

"Or he's never lived here because the Lacey address is the correct one," Mat said darkly.

"Did you and Hamarsson have a fight, sir?" Birdy asked with extra-cheer to her tone.

Turning his head, Mat narrowed his eyes at his deputy. She smirked back at him.

"Touché, Birdy. Touché."

Later that afternoon they had a lot more information on Richard Michael Peterson. Mat had called in Jones and Jorgensen so they would have backup—just in case. What they'd learned about Peterson did not make Mat want to do a happy dance. The dance would come when they had the guy in custody.

Peterson seemed to be a bit of an odd character. There'd been an arrest for assault a few years back, but the charges had been dropped and nothing had ever come of it. There was no permit to carry a conceal weapon. Employment records showed he hadn't stayed in one job for more than a year or two at a time, but they all knew times had been hard. More recently, he'd been unemployed, but he'd finished a certification in auto tech and repair. He did not read like someone Mat thought Hollis would be dating seriously. They didn't have access to Hollis's bank records yet, either, which aggravated Mat.

One thing they did eventually find was a picture of a bearded Rick Peterson and Arsen Hollis on Hollis's Facebook account. The connection had been made, if not yet understood.

Mat sighed. He didn't like what they'd found, but at least they had confirmation there was a link between the two men.

"I could call down to the sushi place and see if they recognize Peterson," Birdy offered. "Maybe Hollis took him there?"

The selfie had been taken at an open-air market of some kind. Mat thought he remembered there were several in Olympia. There was a farmer's market on Piedras as well, but after close inspection, they decided it likely hadn't been taken there. The Piedras market only lasted until mid-September and there were pumpkins and other fall vegetables in the background of the photo.

Mat stared at the driver's license photo again. It was impossible to judge from a picture but to him, Rick Peterson did not seem to match up with the other men Hollis had spent time with. He wasn't well-dressed, flashy, or eye-catchingly attractive. Peterson wasn't a highflier. He was an average-looking guy with sketchy employment and an arrest for assault.

Xavier Stone claimed Hollis had been a user. If that was so, where did Peterson fit in? Mat wanted to close this case and the only way to tie up the loose ends was by talking to Rick Peterson.

"Okay," Mat said, addressing Birdy, Soren, and Jones. It was supposed to be Jones's day off, so Mat felt a little bad, but better more backup than sorry, especially since it was possible Peterson had a weapon. New dad Radden was staying back at the station, ready to respond if anyone called in about gunshots. Mat really hoped Radden didn't move from his chair. "Let's head out and have a chat with Mr. Peterson. Remember, we just want to talk to him, not scare him off. At this point, the connections we have are tenuous. We just want to lay our eyes on him and ask a few questions about Arsen Hollis. The powder residue says Hollis's death was self-inflicted, but the rest of the scene, as you know, isn't adding up."

DMV records indicated that Peterson owned a silver Honda sedan, just like several million other drivers and a bunch of residents on Piedras. Hopefully, Peterson would still be on the island and at home. Four deputies was overkill, but if Peterson was their guy, he would be jumpy.

"If he's home and answers the door, Jones and I will do the talking. No bristling with weapons, just a nice, easygoing sheriff and his deputy who have a few questions. And just in case, we're all wearing vests. Got it?"

They all looked Mat in the eye and nodded.

"Alright, let's go. Birdy, I'll take the lead on the drive over."

THE HOUSE HAD ONCE BEEN part of a farm, but the property had been divided long ago. Surrounded on three sides by a massive laurel hedge, the structure sat a little back from the road and was down the street from Jewel Dairy.

Where Teagan's operation was surrounded by trees so that the property was difficult to see, the front of the Peterson property was open and might have a partial view of the mainland on a nice day.

Mat briefly wondered if Teagan or Benny knew Richard Michael Peterson.

They'd donned their Kevlar vests back at the station. If Peterson was their man, he'd already resorted to using a weapon once that they knew of. In Mat's opinion, that meant it was highly likely he'd use a gun again. Mat wasn't losing a deputy on his watch if he could prevent it.

Arriving quietly and without red and blues, Mat parked along the side of the road not quite in front of the Peterson house and Birdy pulled over a little behind him. Mat squashed down the roil of nerves swirling in his stomach. He'd avoided death almost every day working in the Bay Area and he'd grown used to the quiet and relative safety of his little island. Although he had to admit he'd never been the victim of a car bomb until moving back home.

"Are you ready for this, Deputy?" he asked Jones, shaking off the feeling of unease.

Deputy Jones nodded, his attention toward the house.

"Alright then."

In tandem, Jones and Mat opened their doors and stepped out of the cruiser, meeting the other two deputies at the front of their vehicle.

"Jones and I will knock on the front door," Mat said. "Flynn and Jorgensen, you make your way around to the back. We don't want to have to chase him around the neighborhood if he bolts."

Yes, he'd said all of that back at the station. They could deal with him repeating himself. Mat hoped Peterson was at home. He wanted this over with. His gut was telling him that Peterson was the perp and he needed to be behind bars.

"Let's do this."

As he and Jones began to approach the house, Mat's cell phone vibrated against his thigh. Now was not the time to check the damn thing, but somehow he knew it was Niall. More than once since they'd been together—and a few times before they figured themselves out—they'd called or texted when the other was in a moment of peril. Mat was not a woo-woo guy, not by a long shot, but he slowed his pace as he noted the three steps leading up to the porch and the darkened windows on either side of it.

The house itself was unremarkable. Not run-down but not pristine. The front yard wasn't so overgrown that they couldn't tell where they were stepping and there weren't abandoned vehicles strewn across it. There was no sign of the silver Honda, but there was a smaller building behind the house where a car could be parked.

The little hairs on the back of his neck rose. He hated that he couldn't be sure if the house was empty. There was an abandoned feel to the property, but that could've been because of the time of year.

Then again, it could've been because the resident wanted people to think there was no one inside.

His phone vibrated again, and again, Mat ignored it. He and

Jones kept moving, slowly closing in on the simple porch. Mat flicked his gaze to one of the front windows that looked out into the yard. They were covered, but had he seen a shadow inside?

Was someone waiting on the other side of the door? A someone who'd already murdered once? A cornered beast wouldn't hesitate to strike out again. Mat peered at the window, and this time he was certain he saw movement behind one of the shades.

Instinct kicked in. "Drop and roll," Mat yelled.

Thank fuck Jones listened. They hit the ground hard. Mat rolled in one direction and Jones in the other just as the blast of a gun destroyed the door they'd been about to knock on. If they'd waited a second longer, one of them would likely have been mortally injured. As it was, Mat was going to feel the throb of his hip and shoulder for a few days.

Out of the corner of his eye, he saw Birdy and Soren take off running along the edge of the property and toward the back of the house. Then his gaze focused on the black muzzle of a shotgun poking out through the remains of the door.

Mat had a bad feeling about how this was going to end.

"Richard Peterson?" he called out. "Piedras County Sheriff Mat Dempsey. I just want to talk to you."

"Fuck you."

Mat looked over at Jones, who nodded his head toward the steps. The deputy had ended up near a leggy hydrangea bush, so it was possible Peterson couldn't see him.

"I'd like to talk to you about Arsen Hollis," Mat yelled.

"Arsen Hollis," the speaker—Mat was going to assume it was Rick Peterson—scoffed.

"Mr. Peterson, would you be willing to put the gun aside so we can have a conversation?"

Mat moved as if he was going to rise to his feet. The muzzle swung toward him.

"Stay where you are!"

Jones used the distraction to scoot closer to the house, but still out of range of the gunman.

"Both of you fucking cops stay where you are! If you move another inch, I'll blow your fucking heads off."

Mat motioned for Jones to stay put. This situation was what Mat had feared the most, that Peterson wanted to go out in a blaze of gunfire. Suicide by cop. Had Peterson spotted Birdy and Soren? Did he know there were not two but four law officers on his property? If Peterson hadn't been looking out the window when they arrived, he might have assumed two cruisers equaled two cops. He was grasping at straws, he knew, but these deputies were his family. He didn't want anyone hurt.

"Alright, let's not let things get out of hand. We just want to talk to you. Can I stand up so I'm not rolling in the mud?"

He needed to keep Peterson's attention on him and Jones and away from what might be happening at the back of the house.

Away from Birdy and Soren.

DAKOTA

"Well, that could have been worse," Niall commented as he tossed his cell phone in the cup holder and slid behind the wheel. "It could've gone on even longer."

"It wasn't that bad." Dakota let out a small chuckle. He was starting to understand that grumpy was a default for his half brother. Much like it was for himself.

Even Dakota could tell that Niall liked the people they'd had lunch with. And the meeting for the memorial hadn't been horrible. Weird, yes. Unsettling, definitely. But not horrible. He'd liked Cody Prescott immediately and Sage was one of those people who put people at ease just by being in the same room.

"What?" Niall exclaimed. "Did they get to you when I left you alone and went to the men's room?"

"Sage was easy to talk to. She had some good suggestions," Dakota said with a shrug. "I think I will probably say something Saturday, but she reminded me that I don't have to decide beforehand."

Even though Ana had left him behind, Dakota didn't want people who'd known her to think his life had been entirely terrible. And the only person who could make sure that didn't happen was him. Speaking up was more for him than it was for his mother.

"Yeah, Sage is good people. So are Shay, Cody, and Ryder. Don't tell them I said so."

Dakota was sure that both Cody Prescott and Ryder Mann knew that Niall liked and respected them. He shifted in his seat, gearing himself up to ask the question that had been on his mind since Niall showed up in Collier's Creek.

"Um, what do you know about Mom's case?"

Almost-nightmares had been haunting his sleep since Niall had waltzed into Jake's Pub and informed him of Ana's fate. When Dakota had finally called the detective in Barstow and talked to her, she'd been pleasant but she didn't have much to say that didn't sound practiced.

Dakota didn't particularly want to think about how his mother died. Or where her body had been discovered. But if he wanted a career in law enforcement, he had to learn to ask the hard questions, didn't he? Even if they were personal.

Niall glanced down at his phone again, as if he was expecting a text or call any minute. Dakota could see there were no notifications on the screen. Niall huffed and then, looking over his shoulder, backed out of the parking spot.

"Ana's file," Niall said in a musing tone. "Well, there's not much. Not much at all. The initial investigator did a good job with what was found at the scene."

"I talked to Detective Garcia," Dakota told him, "after you left."

Again, Tad had nagged him into it. Telling Dakota he should talk to the detectives in California himself instead of getting the information secondhand. Tad was sometimes right, which was always irritating.

"Good. So Garcia filled you in?"

"I guess. I was hoping you could tell me more."

They turned onto the road in front of the resort. "Are you sure you're ready to hear this?"

No, he wasn't. And by the way Niall quickly glanced at him, he knew it too. Was there ever a good time to talk about the murder of someone you knew?

"I'm positive."

If he couldn't handle the truth about his own mother, how could he be a good investigator himself? Watching Niall with the rest of the people—except for Shay, who was a lawyer, and there seemed to be a story there—and interacting with them during lunch had been eye-opening for Dakota. After sitting down, Dakota had had to force himself not to react to every little comment, every glance his direction. Mat Dempsey was right. This situation wasn't just happening to him, it was happening to Niall too. Niall hadn't asked for a new half brother to randomly appear in his life.

He was still angry though. Very angry. But it wasn't directed at Niall Hamarsson. It was at his mom for putting herself in perilous situations and repeatedly seeking out people who took advantage of her. Why did she have to be like that? What had driven her to behave recklessly? Even before they moved to Wyoming, Dakota had memories of her letting him stay over at friends' houses for entire weekends when he'd still been in kindergarten. What had she been doing while he was gone?

Now he thought he knew, and it made him sad for Ana. Sad for himself too but mostly for Ana, who'd never found what she was looking for.

"The medical examiner's report stated she'd been dead for anywhere between around thirty-six hours and twelve days," said Niall. "The window of time is wide because the unexpected rain played havoc with the remains and interfered with any evidence that might have been left behind. Officially, the cause of death was strangulation but to be honest, there's no way even to know that for sure."

Dakota nodded, peering out the window at the trees and shrubs along the side of the road. It was easier to talk that way. "That's what the detective told me too."

"I don't think she was murdered where she was discovered," Niall said. "The culvert was just a handy place to stash her body."

Like throwing trash out a car window on the freeway.

Dakota shoved the image aside. "How do you manage it?"

"Manage what?"

"The hard stuff. Cases like... this one."

He'd had to take a couple of psychology courses for his degree, but what was a class to real-life experience? Sheriff Morgan had even let him do some ride-alongs with him for class experience, but all they'd done was pull a few people over for speeding and give Geraldine a lecture when her damn dog got loose for the hundredth time.

Niall didn't immediately answer. Dakota waited. Eventually, Niall cleared his throat and began, "When I was a young cop, around your age, I wasn't in a good head space." He snorted. "Understatement of the year. But I think it made me good at my job. Not giving a fuck about anything but the facts that led to the truth meant I wasn't distracted by the other bullshit. I focused on what I could control and that was how I solved cases."

When Niall was starting his career, Dakota had been a baby, a newborn even. Had their mom known her firstborn was a police officer? She'd never once said anything that hinted there was an older brother somewhere in the world. But that didn't mean she hadn't known what Niall had grown up to be. Maybe she hadn't even known Niall was alive.

"My single-mindedness made me a good cop and investigator; I think it did anyway. I've always had a strong belief that 'to protect and serve' means to protect and serve all the community, no matter who they are. The dead deserve as much attention as the living. The poor, the rich, et cetera. But I haven't answered your question, have I? I don't really manage it, I suppose. I retired, didn't I? Mat does a lot to keep my demons at bay. But mostly I just fully intend to solve every case I possibly can. Justice is my focus."

"But Mom's case is impossible."

"Not impossible, but highly improbable. Yes, it's been a long time, and there wasn't much evidence to start with. But I'm going to go over the file again with a fine-tooth comb. There could be something Black missed, but I don't want you getting your hopes up that there'll be an arrest."

"Yeah." Dakota nodded, then added, "I love Wyoming, but I don't think it felt like home to Mom. Why do you think she never tried to come back here?"

A sweeping curve dumped them onto the road that led toward Mat and Niall's house. Soon enough they'd be passing through the three-horse town of Killegan's Point.

"I can't begin to guess where Ana's head was. Od and Jo—our grandparents—would have been happy to take you in, although I think Od had already passed by the time you were born. I'm sorry you never got to meet them." Niall quickly glanced at Dakota and then back at the road. "You and I inherited a lot of the Hamarsson genes."

"Yeah, I saw that in some of the photos. Maybe it's best Mom didn't come back here. Maybe she knew she couldn't stay clean or whatever and didn't want to bring that part of herself here?"

Niall didn't answer right away; his focus looked to be on the road ahead of them. A car turned out of a driveway and headed away from them, toward Hidden Harbor. A minute later,

Dakota spotted the weird pink building that seemed to be a grocery store. Someone was up on a ladder changing the sales on the reader board.

"You could be right. Maybe she never came home because she was afraid *and* ashamed. Humans are damn hard on themselves sometimes."

Abruptly, they both heard a wailing sound. Seconds later, a cop car was speeding toward them with its lights and siren blaring.

Niall slowed and pulled to the right but before it reached them, the car turned left and disappeared down a street just past the store.

"What. The. Fuck," Niall growled.

NIALL

Snatching his phone up from the console, Niall repeatedly jabbed his index finger against the Call button. He'd texted Mat earlier, after wrapping up with Sage and Cody, but Mat hadn't replied. Mat didn't answer this time either. A frisson of dread crept up his spine and spread out across his shoulders, leaving him almost breathless. Tossing the phone down. Niall pulled out onto the road again.

"Don't do what I'm about to do," he told Dakota. "And when we get there, don't follow me. Stay in the fucking car."

He slammed on the gas pedal and the car jerked forward. By the time he reached the right turn, they were going forty and Niall tapped the brakes as he took the corner too fast. A fifteen-year-old Subaru Outback wasn't exactly meant for pursuit.

Down the street a couple hundred yards were two PCSD cruisers parked along the side of the road. The sheriff's car they'd seen was pulled to a stop in the middle of the road and the driver's side door swung open.

Niall recognized Deputy Radden immediately. Radden looked back up the street at them and motioned for Niall to stop. Niall didn't stop. He kept going until he was even with Radden and opened his window.

"What's going on, Deputy Radden?" he demanded.

Radden had a few more years of experience under his belt than when Niall had first met him, but he was still a small-town cop who'd never dealt with much more than an irate driver trying to cut the ferry line. And wasn't he on paternity leave? No, he was recently back on duty, Niall thought.

"Um, sir, Mr. Hamarsson, I need to ask that you stay away from the scene."

"Radden, look at me. Look me in the eyes," Niall growled soft and low.

Radden turned his head and briefly glanced at Niall before returning his attention to a white house on the right side of the street. From his vantage point in the Subaru, Niall couldn't see what was going on, but Mat's cruiser was something he recognized on sight.

"Do I look like I'm going anywhere, Radden?"

Radden's head moved almost imperceptivity. "No, sir."

"Alright, then. I'm getting out of my car now. I'm coming to stand next to you. When I do, how about you tell me what the fuck is going on here?"

Flicking the lock on his door, Niall stepped out onto the pavement and moved to stand shoulder to shoulder with Deputy Radden. From there, he saw two figures laying on the ground in front of the house.

"Who's on the ground and are they injured?"

"Sheriff Dempsey, sir, and Deputy Jones, sir. As far as I know, they are not injured. The suspect did fire a shot from inside the house, sir."

Niall saw there was a gaping hole in the front door.

"Where's Deputy Flynn?"

Birdy was the most levelheaded deputy Mat had, although Niall respected the hell out of Jorgensen as well.

"I don't know for certain. The uh, suspect, won't let the sheriff use his radio. Sherriff Dempsey had me wait at the station ready to respond if calls about gunshots came in. I saw him try when I arrived, but the suspect became very agitated."

"Have you radioed Flynn and Jorgensen?"

"It's radio silence, sir. I think they're trying to gain access through the back of the house."

Okay, that was good. There was hope this could be settled without violence. Niall sucked in a lungful of oxygen, trying to calm himself down.

"Have you assessed his demands?"

"His what, sir?"

"What does this guy want? Even if he doesn't know what it is, he wants something. Buy some time for the team, distract him. Get out your bullhorn and find out what he wants."

"Uh, okay, sir."

Moving quickly, Radden popped the cruiser's trunk and rummaged around for a few seconds, finally emerging with a white bullhorn. He stared at it and then at Niall.

"Well? What are you waiting for?"

Radden seemed to shake himself out of a daze and flipped the power switch, and the megaphone powered up with an earsplitting screech that echoed down the street. After taking a few steps closer to the house, Radden lifted the thing up and began to speak.

"Um..."

The speaker tweaked again. Niall winced and briefly shut his eyes. "For fuck's sake."

Radden rallied. "This is the Piedras County Sheriff's Department," he said. "I'm Deputy Radden. Please put the weapon down and come out of the house. We want this to end peacefully."

"Good start. Tell him we don't mean any harm, we just want to talk to him."

Although, if Niall ever got his hands on the man, he was going to learn that Niall's definition of harm was ever-changing.

"We don't mean you any harm," Radden said. "We just need to talk to you."

There was no immediate response from whoever was inside the house. Niall thought he saw a shadow move, but it was hard to be certain.

"Good job. We need to keep him distracted. I have the feeling that Flynn and Jorgensen must have run into some trouble in the back. Keep him talking, keep his attention on us."

"Talk about what?" Radden whispered.

"Ask him open-ended questions," Dakota said from behind Niall.

Niall spun around at the voice and noted that Dakota had not stayed in the car as he'd been directed. The kid shrugged. "I just took a class with a section on hostage negotiation. You're supposed to ask open-ended questions and give them time to answer. Ask what he's upset about and listen to what he replies."

"Do it," Niall prodded the deputy.

Radden raised the horn to his lips again. "Can you tell us what you're upset about and how we can help you?"

"No one, no one can help me," the man shouted back. "Hollis ruined me. I didn't do anything."

"Don't answer right away," Dakota whispered. "There needs to be pauses, give him time."

The ensuing pause was several lifetimes long. Niall hated situations like this. Luckily, he'd only been involved in a few crisis situations over his career. His "clients" were already dead when he got involved. Today, however, Niall's focus was on his husband, the sheriff, who was in the direct line of fire should the perp suddenly decide enough was enough.

"Suicide by cop is the last thing we need, Radden. Keep him talking."

"We can help you, Mr. Peterson," the deputy said. "Just tell us what you need right now."

"There's nothing. There's nothing anyone can do..."

Those four words froze the blood in Niall's veins and his heart skipped several beats. This was not the direction anyone wanted Peterson heading.

But before anyone could react, or Niall could direct Radden to say something more to keep Peterson's attention on them and not Mat or the weapon he held, he heard Birdy yell, "Freeze!"

Muffled thuds and thumps accompanying the louder sound of something crashing and shattering inside reached Niall's ears. Maybe more than one something. Niall imagined it was a curio cabinet or something like that. Perhaps the guy collected creepy porcelain cat dolls.

Leaping up off the ground, Mat ran up the stairs into the house, the other deputy—Jones, Niall thought— right behind him. Niall braced himself for the sound of gunfire, but it never came. The three of them on the sidelines—and probably every neighbor in the area—held their breath, waiting to see what would happen next.

A few minutes passed before Mat and Soren emerged together. The man who Niall assumed was Peterson was secured between them. His hands were cuffed behind his back and his head hung low. Flynn and Jones followed them, Jones brushing mud and grass off the front of his uniform.

Straightening to his full height, Niall caught Mat's bright gaze with his own. He was rewarded with an almost invisible chin nod. Mat was fine. No one had been hurt. There'd be some conversation later tonight, probably about how Niall needed to stay away from active scenes, but at least Niall could breathe again.

"It must be hard being in a relationship with a law officer," Dakota said slowly as if the thought had just struck him.

"It's fucking hard," Niall agreed somberly.

MAT

Mat was beyond exhausted when he finally walked through the door of his and Niall's home that night. His shoulder ached from when he'd hit the ground in front of Peterson's house, and the Advil he'd swallowed down at the station hadn't done much more than dull the pain.

It was close to midnight. The processing of Peterson had taken several hours and even though Mat believed him when he said he hadn't murdered Arsen Hollis, that Arsen had turned the gun on himself, there were still lawyers involved—as there should be when a person threatens an officer—and Mat had decided a 24/7 suicide watch was in order. Niall wasn't going to be happy when Mat left again at four in the morning.

"What are you doing there?" he asked the hulking form sprawled along the length of their couch. Fenrir wagged his tail and appeared to grin at him but didn't bother slithering off the couch to the floor where he belonged.

"Oh, you know, exercising his canine rights," Niall said from the kitchen table where Dakota was sitting in the chair next to him.

"Why are you guys still up?" Mat asked.

Dakota gave Mat a sideways glance. "It's only 11:30."

Right. Because Mat was officially An Old Man who liked to be in bed early when he could.

"Ah, to be young again," he quipped, peeling off his jacket and untying his shoes so he could toe them off. "What are you two doing?"

Papers were spread across the table and both of them had what looked to be empty cups of coffee at their elbows. A few of the papers had ring marks where a mug had undoubtedly been set down on them, a hallmark of Niall working late—or early.

"The Doe case I've been working on. I figured I'd give Dakota a stab at it. He's had some interesting ideas. I might run one or two of them past the team tomorrow."

"Only you would bond over a cold case, Niall. I'm changing into my pajamas. I have to be back at the station at four a.m. to relieve Soren."

Niall frowned at the news that Mat would be out of their bed extra early.

"Once we got to the station, Peterson started talking," Mat told them. "Apparently, he'd figured out that Hollis was only interested in the property he had inherited here and not him. Peterson told him no way was he selling it and got out of the car for some air. When he came back, Hollis had shot himself."

A smug expression flitted across Niall's face. Mat allowed himself to roll his eyes.

"We'll never know the whole story, but they had been fighting and Peterson says Hollis owned a gun and that he kept it in the glove compartment. The gun is at the bottom of the harbor now. When he came back from his walk and found him, Peterson panicked and tossed it, thinking he would end up taking the blame. Then he took one of the orange vests from a storage closet and blended in until he could just walk off."

"The closets are right there by the cars," Niall said thoughtfully, "and I swear the doors are unlocked or even swinging wide open half the time, so I can see that being true. But why did he go to all this trouble? Why not just call you guys when he found the body?"

"There are definitely more questions that need to be asked. I think he's telling the truth, but now it's up to people at a higher paygrade than me."

Mat eyed Dakota. "Cone of silence. This is off-the-record information."

Dakota nodded solemnly. "I won't say anything."

"Secrets. Another reason it's hard having a partner in law enforcement," Niall said.

"I'm hitting the sack," Mat announced. "Four is going to come early."

Standing up from the table, Niall said, "I'm coming too." He shoveled the papers back into the manila file folder and stacked it onto a pile in the middle of the table.

IN THE DARK of their bedroom, Niall ran his hands across Mat's chest and down his side. "You promise you're okay?"

"I'm fine," Mat murmured. "Yes, my shoulder hurts like hell, but it will pass. I'm fine. No one got hurt today. We brought Peterson in. All is good in the Hamarsson-Dempsey world. That tickles, so knock it off. I need to get some sleep."

Niall scooted over but still somehow managed to drape his larger body across Mat's. Mat turned onto his good shoulder and moved backward so Niall could be the big spoon. A strong arm wrapped around his waist and pulled him even closer.

"I didn't like seeing you lying on the ground," Niall whispered in his ear.

Mat was tempted to remind him that he shouldn't have followed Radden to the scene. But honestly, if their roles had been reversed, Mat would've done the same. The same rules just didn't apply to Mat and Niall.

WHEN HE OPENED his eyes again, Niall was still wrapped around him.

"I've gotta get up, babe. Neither of us want to listen to Dany bitch about Soren's hours the next time we see him."

Niall rolled over onto his back. "Dany thinks he's scary. But I'm scarier."

"Yeah, yeah, big guy. You just keep telling yourself that," Mat retorted. "Do you want me to start the coffee pot or just make a single cup?"

"Start the pot. I won't be able to go back to sleep without you in the bed."

Opening their closet door, Mat grabbed a fresh uniform and dressed before heading out to the main room. Niall *was* tough and scary up until he said things like "I can't sleep without you."

Mat quietly slipped out of the room, a smile curving his lips.

DAKOTA

It was raining. Not the pelting rain he experienced in Wyoming. This was a seemingly light, misty rain that had Dakota's barn coat heavy with the damp in just minutes.

The weather seemed appropriate. His mother's long overdue memorial was set to begin in half an hour. Looking around, Dakota counted ten people aside from himself, Niall, and Mat.

"Maybe the weather will keep them away," grumbled Niall from where he was hunched in an expensive-looking waterproof rain jacket with the hood pulled over his head. If Dakota squinted, he resembled a grouchy bear who shopped at REI.

"Don't count on it," Mat said. "This is a big event, and you know it." Mat was bundled up too.

The weather didn't bother Dakota, but it did seem like late March was planning on making April work hard if flowers were going to bloom or the ground dry out.

Dakota had his hands jammed into the deep pockets of his coat. When his phone vibrated, he felt it under his fingertips. Stepping aside to stand under the relative protection of a huge cedar tree, he pulled it out and pressed Accept.

"What?"

"Hey, it's Tad."

"Tad, you do know you're the only one who calls me, right?"

Dakota did have a few other friends, but Tad was the only one he answered the phone for.

"Ah, well. Are you okay? Has it started yet?"

Dakota was watching a circa 1975 Cadillac pull into the Brooch parking lot. Shay was behind the wheel. One of the back doors opened, and Ryder Mann emerged. Shutting his door, Ryder moved to the passenger door and opened it.

An older woman sat in the front seat. She had absolutely pure white hair and when she turned her head, Dakota saw she wore a pair of black cats-eye glasses. Ryder gave her his arm and helped her out of the car. He said something, Dakota couldn't hear what, only to have her swat at his shoulder. Smiling and unperturbed, Ryder kissed her on the cheek. Reaching back into the car, Ryder pulled out an umbrella and opened it over her.

Whoever she was, she was tiny and old. Her clothing was protected by a long, black raincoat, but Dakota suspected she was impeccably dressed underneath it.

"Dakota?"

"What?" He pulled his attention away from the senior citizen and back to the phone call. "Oh. No, it hasn't started yet."

"Call me when it's over if you need to."

"Sure, okay. Sorry, some more people just got here and I should probably get off the phone."

"It's going to be fine."

"It's going to be over soon, and I won't have to think about it anymore," Dakota corrected.

"Maybe the memorial will be over soon, but I bet you keep thinking about what happened to your mom."

"I know you're right, Tad. But do you always have to be right?"

Tad just laughed. "Yes? When're you coming back? Pete's been asking. I told him to fuck off, that you're allowed family leave, but you know how he is."

"Tell him I'll be back home by the end of the week. Are we allowed family leave?"

"I have no idea, but it sounded good at the time."

Clicking off, Dakota shoved his phone away. The older woman was making her way across the grass to where he stood. She kept herself steady by holding onto Shay's forearm. They stopped in front of him and she looked him up and down. Dakota felt a bit like he was on display and she was deciding whether he was worth the price of admission.

"So, you're my newest great-grandson," she said.

"I am?" He looked at Shay. Mat and Niall hadn't said anything about another relative.

"Technically, no," Shay said. "But I think Claribel is planning on an honorary title for you. Dakota Green, this is Claribel Delacombe, my and Niall's great-aunt. Don't take anything she says personally or as fact of any kind. And don't play bingo with her."

"Um, it's nice to meet you, Mrs.—"

"None of that crap, just call me Claribel. Shay told me a little about you. Sounds like you've had quite the shock." She swatted at Shay's arm. "No need to scare him off bingo, nephew."

"Claribel and her cronies are padding their retirement with bingo winnings," Shay said. "They are ruthless and prey on the unsuspecting."

"Hmph," Claribel sniffed. "Anyway, it's a pleasure to meet you even if it's under unfortunate circumstances. I knew your mother, although not for long, seeing as how she left so young.

I'm sure David, my useless nephew and Shay's and Niall's father, kept her tucked away so none of us would figure out what was happening. And right under our noses too. It's obvious you're a Hamarsson, you're a spitting image of our Niall."

"Our Niall" heard her comment and, Dakota thought, rolled his eyes.

"I'm sure it's nice to meet you too," Dakota said.

"Oh," she huffed out with a laugh, "I doubt that, but I tend to grow on people. Come with us, let's get this thing over with—I mean started."

Shay bit his lip and shook his head at Claribel's words.

"Again, don't take anything she says personally."

"Noted. It's not as if Niall hasn't said that seven times already. And that's just today," Dakota responded. He walked with the group toward the beach where they were speaking and releasing Ana's ashes. He did like Claribel. Her attitude was refreshing.

AT THE BEACH, Dakota and Niall stood next to each other, with Mat on the other side of Niall. In the end, the biting wind made it almost impossible to hear what anyone was saying—not that many had anything to say.

"I've done this once already, a few years ago. It's your turn now to set Ana free," Niall said to Dakota. "The tide is heading out so now is the time."

Niall set a handmade wooden Viking-style longboat on the rocks and sand in front of Dakota and close to the tide line. The boat was simple, about two feet long, no sails or anything. Dakota knew some of Ana's ashes were inside the hull as well as scraps of paper with messages written on them.

In Dakota's case, he'd kept it simple. *I hope you're happy now, Mom.*

"It's probably too windy to stay lit, but here's a lighter." Mat drew one of those long barbecue-lighting sticks out from his coat pocket and handed it to Dakota.

With everyone watching him, Dakota crouched down and clicked the lighter several times before a small flame appeared. He carefully set it against the twine wrapped around the boat. Mat was right, at first it didn't want to burn. But Dakota clicked and held the igniter, and tentative flames eventually began licking along the twine.

"I may have doused the thing in lighter fluid," Niall said so only Mat and Dakota could hear him. "Some big waves are starting to come in."

They all took several steps back as the waves rolled toward them and up the beach, splashing against the boat. The flames flickered out, but the boat was lifted up onto the surface of the seawater. And when the waves slid backward, they took Ana with them.

Dakota watched for as long as he could distinguish the boat from the dark waters surrounding Piedras Island. At one point, he thought he saw flames flare up again, but it was probably a figment of his imagination.

"I don't know about you, but I'm cold and getting damp and the rest of these weirdos aren't going inside until we do," said Niall.

"I'm ready," Dakota replied. "Let's go."

"I'VE HAD ABOUT enough peopling for the rest of the year," Niall griped as the three of them tromped into Mat and Niall's house after the memorial. "I'm turning off my phone and not answering the door if someone knocks."

It was early evening and Dakota was also tired of people, even though he'd liked most everyone he'd met that day.

"Good luck with that," Mat scoffed. "Would you rather have Ryder on the phone or at our door? If you don't answer a call, you know he'll come over. And he won't go away until he gets what he wants. I have to say, tenacity is just one of the many things I like about him."

"Yeah, I suppose he has his good points."

Dakota waited while Niall hung his coat up and then he did the same. Mat did not move to hang his.

Niall narrowed his eyes and shot a dark glance in the sheriff's direction. "You have to go in?"

"Yep." Mat nodded. "Peterson's lawyer has finally arrived. I need to be there."

A gusty sigh escaped Niall.

"Call if it goes late."

"So... you are going to answer your phone?"

"I always answer calls from you and you know it."

Mat definitely looked smug at Niall's response.

Dakota decided he needed to go to the bathroom and give the two men some space. When he came back out, Mat had left and Niall was sitting at the table.

Niall looked over at him. "I need to get the dog outside, but I've had enough outdoors for the time being."

They both glanced across the room. Fenrir was sacked out on the couch with the cat curled up next to him. The dog didn't appear to care about the out of doors at the moment.

Niall gestured at the paperwork in front of him. "Are you interested in looking over Ana's file? Fresh eyes and all that."

The last time Niall had asked him that question, Dakota had refused. After speaking with Detective Garcia, he hadn't been ready to see the crime scene photographs he knew were in the file. But today, now that Ana's remains had been put to rest, the timing felt right.

"You don't have to," Niall assured him. "You never have to

see them. I have a lifetime's experience of not allowing myself to be affected by crime scene photos. It's not easy, especially when you're familiar with the person."

Dakota pulled out a chair and sat down.

"I want to."

"Okay." Not questioning him further, Niall pushed the papers across the table.

A quick glance told Dakota they'd been printed from photographs of the original paperwork. The first page appeared to be a summary; he scanned it and flipped to the next page.

"Read it over and tell me what you think."

Dakota nodded and began to read.

From his phone conversation with the Barstow detective, he knew the basics of how his mom had been discovered and that there were no leads. A rainy night had meant flooding roadways. Some kind of maintenance worker had called the cops when he thought he'd seen a human body inside a culvert.

The detective called to the scene had confirmed the discovery and brought in an evidence collection team. There hadn't been much for them to find though, and the case had stalled before there was hope of catching the fucker who'd murdered Ana Green. Doing his best to read through the file dispassionately, Dakota plowed on. He even looked at the photographs.

Minutes later, Dakota found himself tapping one of the sheets with his index finger.

"What?" Niall asked.

"Probably nothing."

"Tell me anyway."

"Did you ever see that Tom Hanks movie, Castaway?"

Niall waggled his head, which Dakota was going to assume was a no.

"Well, Mom loved it. She was a huge Tom Hanks fan. I was

pretty young the first time I saw it, like five or six. If Mom didn't have plans to go out, she would rent movies from this crappy video store near us when we lived in Barstow. In the movie, this guy is in a plane crash and all he ends up having for a friend is a Wilson volleyball."

Niall raised a skeptical eyebrow.

"A volleyball? Who writes this stuff?"

"It's a good movie, and bear with me here. Like I said, Mom loved the movie. So when she started dating a guy whose last name was Wilson, it stuck with me."

"Wilson?" Niall dragged the papers back across the table and flipped through them until he found the page Dakota had been tapping. The one with the name of the maintenance worker. Jack Wilson.

"Jack Wilson?"

Dakota nodded. "I didn't like him much. He had no sense of humor. I don't really remember much about him except that he didn't think it was funny when I ran around yelling *Wilson, Wilson!* the first time I learned his name. You have to see the movie to understand."

"Jack Wilson isn't an uncommon name. He came back the next day to give a statement," Niall mused. "The original detective even said something about his name when I talked to him. Anything else you remember about him? Did he stick with Ana? Did they fight? Did he creep you out?"

Dakota did his best to recall Jack Wilson. "Like I said, I didn't like him much, I guess. He never hurt me or anything, but"—a memory Dakota had long buried came hurtling back—"I remember I had this stuffed animal. Stitch, from the movie."

Niall shook his head and Dakota briefly wondered if his half brother had actually lived under a rock for most of his life. For fuck's sake, Dakota lived in Wyoming and was more in touch.

"Anyway, before we moved away, he gave me this big

lecture about how boys didn't sleep with dolls. How I needed to learn to be a real man. I remember it because I was so scared. He was getting in my face about it. Mom didn't care about my Stitch doll, my friends didn't care. We all had stuffed animals, it was no big deal. The big deal was that Stitch disappeared off my bed while I was at school. I searched all over and found it torn up and stuffed in the kitchen trash. He hadn't even tried to hide it."

"Thus establishing that, if nothing else, he was an asshole," Niall said.

"Yeah. I was completely distraught and told Mom what had happened. She hadn't been home, maybe she'd been at work, asked him to watch me until she got home. That part I don't remember."

"Anything else?"

"He might have stuck around for a little while longer, I'm not sure. But it also seems like we maybe just up and moved pretty soon afterward. Mom suddenly had a new job as a cook and it came with housing for both of us. One day we were in Barstow and the next we were living on a ranch in the middle of nowhere. We moved around a lot. She would hear about a job in a new town and then we'd move. I got used to being the new kid constantly. Until Wyoming."

Niall was silent, clearly processing what Dakota had told him about their mom and Jack Wilson. It seemed to Dakota that it was a long shot. Probably it had just been coincidence that the person who found her body had the same name.

"I don't believe in coincidence. Not when it comes to murder," Niall said, echoing Dakota's thoughts. He jabbed his index finger at the paper. "Jack Wilson was involved. Get your coat on, we're going to Ryder's."

· · ·

RYDER AND SHAY'S home was a mansion.

"Jesus," Dakota breathed out the word.

"Yeah, Shay's a go big or go home kind of guy and he has the money. He inherited the land when David died but waited to build on it. The best part, though, is that he had a state-of-the-art computer system installed per Ryder's specs. If anyone can find the Jack Wilson we are looking for, it'll be Ryder."

"Is this a case of using his powers for good?" Dakota asked.

"It absolutely is. Don't get your hopes up though. The guy could be dead, in prison already, living under an alias—although that's harder these days unless you go completely off the grid. It's a bit of a needle in a haystack situation, and we may not find him."

Dakota crossed his fingers that they did.

EVEN THOUGH IT was after eight in the evening, Ryder was happy to see them when he opened the front door. And when Niall explained what he and Dakota needed, Ryder rubbed his hands together with glee.

"I've been wanting to test some software I developed. This is perfect. Shay, we have visitors," Ryder called out. "Come, this way."

Dakota hardly noted the living room and kitchen as he and Niall followed Ryder through both rooms and then down an open, curving stairway. The daylight basement they ended up in had more electronic equipment than Dakota had ever seen in his life. It looked like something from a Hollywood TV show. He counted four monitors at first glance.

"Coffees?" Shay asked from the top of the stairs.

A grunt from Niall as he crowded behind Ryder's chair to watch him work was likely a yes.

"Yeah, that would be great," said Dakota.

"Coming right up."

Dakota stripped off his coat and draped it across the back of a comfortable-looking couch that was strategically placed in the middle of the room. It faced the work area but a person sitting there would also have a view during the daytime. He eased himself down to listen and watch the two West Coast Forensics investigators at work.

It wasn't long before Shay reappeared, carrying a tray with four coffee cups on it. After passing them around, he settled on to the couch next to Dakota.

"It's been a long day, hasn't it?" Shay observed.

Dakota nodded, sipping at the hot liquid. He was exhausted.

"It's been surreal ever since Niall walked into my work and told me he was my half brother."

"Yeah," Shay agreed, "I imagine it was a shock for you. Seeing as we discovered we were related first through a snapshot and then confirmed with testing, I totally get it."

They sat there companionably listening as Ryder typed and chatted and Niall answered with grunts and the occasional, "Well, fuck." Eventually, Shay made his excuses and went upstairs to bed. Dakota set his empty coffee cup down and leaned his head back, planning to shut his eyes for just a few minutes.

When he opened them again, Niall and Ryder were having an intense whispered conversation. And Mat was sitting next to him on the couch. When had he arrived?

"What did I miss?" Dakota asked, trying to shake the grogginess off.

Ryder spun around in his chair to face Dakota.

"I have to preface what I am about to tell you with this statement: Absolutely nothing I did tonight was legal. Mat, cover your ears."

"Consider my ears covered," Mat said.

"Will you get in trouble?" Dakota didn't want Ryder to get arrested because he'd been looking into Ana's death,

"Pfft, I was born for this."

"Tell him what we found out," Niall said impatiently. "What you found out."

"It's not the best news situation, but it's also not the worst." Ryder clicked his mouse and the display brightened, making the room glow.

"Like Detective Black said to Niall, Jack Wilson is a stupidly common name even these days," Ryder commented. "But I thought to myself, how do people meet? Often enough it's at their work. I discovered that Ana worked at a gas station slash truck stop at one point when you lived in Barstow, so what if they met there? And I decided he could either have worked there or was someone who stopped in on a regular basis. I couldn't find any state records of a Jack Wilson working at the same place Ana did, so I started looking at drivers who owned their own rigs. Mostly because it was the easiest place to start. And I stuck to California since that's where Ana was found. Still, it was a lot of people. Thank you, new software."

"That sounds right to me," Dakota said. "I think maybe he drove a big truck."

He heaved himself up and off the couch so he could stretch his legs and wake up. He could see a blue semi-truck cab in his mind's eye. Had it been Wilson's?

"Not to malign the entire fleet of truck drivers who deliver food and goods across this marvelous country," Ryder said, "but I swear there is some kind of serial killer clause in some of their contracts. Anyway, fast forward through a lot of boring dreck to discovering that a Jack Wilson had owned his own truck and an LLC, Wilson Trucking. The time period fit as well. He renewed his license regularly up until about five years ago."

"The bad news, before Ryder gets too carried away with details," Niall interjected, "is that we'll never be able to talk to Wilson. He was arrested, tried, and convicted for killing two women in Southern California. He was rewarded with a life sentence, but the asshole died of kidney disease after only a year inside."

"How did you connect this Jack Wilson to the one Mom knew?" Dakota asked. "How sure are you?"

Not that he was an expert, but this all seemed circumstantial to him.

"Wilson preyed on women in truck stops and rest areas. It was his thing," Ryder told him. "Apparently, he could be charming. If there was car trouble, he'd offer to fix their cars for free and sometimes he even did the work. A survivor who managed to escape Wilson testified at his trial and confirmed she'd been approached at, you guessed it, the same station Ana worked at way back when."

"Okay, so they crossed paths again. Wow."

Dakota didn't know what to think, how to react. Why had his mother gone back to Barstow? Had her demons called her back? That was just one of the questions they would never have an answer to.

"It's my opinion," Niall said, "that he was caught because he wanted to be famous, like the Green River Killer or some other notorious murderer. So he would 'find' the bodies, be a helpful witness, and then move on. Only a savvy detective in Orange County caught on to him."

"He's the guy, I'm all but positive," Ryder stated, pointing at his display. "I know it's not one hundred percent closure, but I think it's as close as we're going to get."

Was this it? Dakota saw the time on the corner of Ryder's screen. 2:05 a.m. and they'd solved Ana's murder. Then he glanced down at the picture Ryder had just pulled up.

Jack Wilson stared back at him.

If Dakota hadn't been convinced before seeing that image, he was now.

"That's him," he whispered. His heart was pounding as if Wilson was in the room with them now, threatening Dakota with a beating if he kept Stitch on his bed. He sucked in a deep breath to calm himself down.

The picture was from the trial. Wilson wore the traditional orange prison jumpsuit and seemed to be staring menacingly at whomever had taken the photograph. Except for his wardrobe, he looked the same as he had when Dakota knew him. Maybe a little older and a little grayer.

And now, dead.

"When investigators caught up with him, they found several high-vis vests in a truck that sounds awfully similar to the one Detective Black described to me when I talked to him."

"So that's it?" Dakota asked no one in particular.

"That's it," Niall confirmed. "I might reach out to the investigator who brought Wilson in and see if he hinted at other killings, but I'm pretty satisfied with what we have. Am I happy that we won't get our day in court? Not at all. But this is a damn sight more than either of us thought we'd ever get."

EPILOGUE

Niall

"NO OFFENSE TO DAKOTA, but I'm glad he's headed back home."

Niall had offered to drive with him and fly back, but Dakota had declined.

"I'm fairly sure Dakota is also glad to be back on the road," Mat replied. "It was nice of you to offer to drive with him."

Fenrir woofed as wavelets drifted up to the beach and then receded again. Hel stood back a little; apparently the wave that had soaked her the other day had her a bit more cautious. The caution would wear off in a few days.

"He invited us to come visit," Niall told Mat.

Dakota probably recognized that Niall didn't want to leave Piedras for a while. Although he was going to have to—the Lindsay trial was officially starting next week.

Mat bumped against his shoulder. "Of course, he did. You're his only family."

Niall stared out at the moody waters of Haro Strait. Today

they reflected the blue sky, puffy clouds, and sunshine over-head. As usual, March was being capricious.

"I told him we couldn't come during the summer. He suggested December. Apparently, there's some holiday festival and it always snows. We could stay in town at the bed-and-breakfast I stayed in when I was there."

Mat didn't immediately answer. Niall turned to look at his husband, whose mouth was hanging open.

"What?"

"Are you getting sentimental on me? Has your hard heart softened?"

"Eh, fuck off." Niall swung his arm over Mat's shoulder, drawing him close. "You're the only one who matters to me."

"I'm not worried. I like the idea of another gruff and rough Hamarsson out there in the world. He's a good kid. We should take him up on it. Maybe make it a family trip? I bet Mom, Ella, and Riley would like it too. We don't get snow worth celebrating here."

"Everybody?"

Mat shrugged. "If they want to. It could be fun. An experi-ence instead of a pile of gifts. Maybe they have sleigh rides there? I think it would mean a lot to Dakota."

Another wave came in, this one dribbling upward across the rocks and sand to barely touch the toe of Niall's boot.

"Tide's changing," he commented.

"Yep, just like it always does."

Niall cocked his head to look at his husband. "Are you giving me crap?"

A pleased smile curved Mat's sexy lips and Niall couldn't help but drop a kiss onto them. When they separated, because a kiss was never just a kiss, Mat said, "Yes, I am giving you crap."

"Never stop."

"I don't plan on it."

"So I guess we're going to Wyoming at the end of the year? I bet Cody knows someone who'd be willing to pet-sit."

"Of course he does."

"I love you, Mat Dempsey."

Niall was the luckiest man in the world to be able to say those words to the man who was his world. He didn't say them often enough.

"And I love you, Niall Hamarsson." Mat ran his hand down Niall's back and squeezed his ass. "Shall we take this inside?"

YES, Dakota gets his turn to fall in love in ***The Map Home***... ask Dakota and he'll say the wall around his heart is high and the moat deep for a reason. Love is a lie.

The Map Home was originally part of the Collier's Creek Christmas series.

IF YOU HAVEN'T ALREADY, check out Real Trouble, Dany and Soren's story and the first in the West Coast Forensics series. Following WCF comes Reclaimed Hearts, beginning with Adverse Conditions.

ABOUT ELLE

Elle's characters are snarky, a tad damaged, and definitely have minds of their own, but the mystery is always solved and hearts crossed. Currently, there are over forty Elle Keaton books available for you to read and many have been produced into audiobooks.

Romantic Suspense and Mystery Romance by Elle Keaton

Shielded Hearts
Veiled Intentions
West Coast Forensics
Reclaimed Hearts
Subtle Deceptions

For more information, to purchase signed paperbacks or audio, please visit my direct sales website

ElleKeatonAuthor

Thank you for supporting this indie author!

AFTERWORD

This is a work of fiction, created without use of AI technology. Any names, characters, places or incidents are products of the author's imagination and used in a fictitious manner. Any resemblance to actual people, places, or events is purely coincidental or fictional.

Elle Keaton's creative body of work cannot be used in any manner for the purpose of training AI.

The author, Elle Keaton, supports the right of humans to control their artistic works. No part of this book has been created using AI-generated images or narrative, as known by the author. The primary style sources used in the writing of this book are the online versions of the Merriam-Webster Dictionary and The Chicago Manual of Style. Due to their inherent limitations for fiction-writing and the author's personal style choices, there are instances where other style guide rules have been consistently applied. Region-based idioms, age- or era-appropriate slang, UK spelling and style rules, and other deviations based on specific dialects may inform some of these choices. Should you have questions, please contact the author at: dirty dogpress@gmail.com

www.ingramcontent.com/pod-product-compliance
Lightning Source LLC
Chambersburg PA
CBHW070937010826
48976CB00028B/2402